THE OPHELIA KILLER

Also by Valerie Geary

Crooked River

Everything We Lost

Brett Buchanan Mystery Series:
On A Dark Tide (Book 1)
The Ophelia Killer (A Prequel)
Edge of the Storm (Book 2)

THE OPHELIA KILLER

BRETT BUCHANAN MYSTERY SERIES

A PREQUEL

VALERIE GEARY

This is a work of fiction. Names, characters, places, and incidents either are the product of the author's imagination or are used fictitiously. Any resemblance to actual events, locales, organizations, or persons, living or dead, is entirely coincidental.

THE OPHELIA KILLER

First edition August 2021

ISBN 978-1-954815-04-9

www.valeriegeary.com

To everyone who has ever
loved a very good dog.

Author's Note

The Ophelia Killer is a standalone prequel to the Brett Buchanan Mystery Series. The narrative takes place four years prior to the start of Book 1 in the series, *On A Dark Tide*. Though chronologically a prequel, I wrote *The Ophelia Killer* with the hope that it could be read at any point that you, Dear Reader, discovered these characters. Whether you have already been introduced to Brett Buchanan or are finding her for the first time, I hope you enjoy reading *The Ophelia Killer* and all the rest of the books in the series.

Book 1: *On A Dark Tide* is currently available to purchase through all major online retailers or you can buy the book directly from my online store: www.valeriegeary.com

Thank you for reading!

THE OPHELIA KILLER

CHAPTER 1

In his six years working as a reporter for the *Statesman Journal*, Jimmy Eagan has never been the first person to arrive at a scene. Usually, by the time he shows up, it's already too late. The tape is stretched, the cops are swarming, and the bodies are bagged. Today, the location that the dispatcher broadcasts over the scanner is an easy, ten minute drive from his apartment.

As he parks beside a cut-grass field baked yellow in the summer heat, a jolt of adrenaline floods through him at the thought of what kind of story he'll be able to write with such unrestricted access. He grabs his press badge and camera and skids down the slight embankment into the field, moving toward a distant clump of spindly trees where he knows the dead girl waits.

The Marion County dispatcher didn't give many details. Someone reported finding a body in a patch of woods near Crocker Creek, and the closest Salem police officer was asked to respond. It was this lack of information, paired with the fact that it's nearing the end of August, that sent Jimmy racing from his apartment at seven o'clock in the morning before he even had his first cup of coffee.

Now he walks carefully, double-checking where he puts his

feet, hoping he's wrong about this one. Maybe the body isn't another young woman, but a farmer out for a walk who collapsed in the heat. Or a drifter who stepped into the trees to take a piss, and fate handed him a heart attack instead. Or ancient bones from an ancient death, the earth giving them up now because of last spring's heavy rainfall and the shifting of time and tectonic plates. But then Jimmy reaches the edge of the trees and the trickle of water that defines Crocker Creek. It's here on the muddy banks where he finds the flowers.

Dried out husks of weeds, a mix of cow parsnips, aster, yarrow, and grass stalks pulled from the field nearby, ripped up by the roots and bound with a pale blue ribbon. It's the same robin's egg shade of blue as the ribbon found wrapped around the stems of another wildflower bouquet discovered near another dead girl last August, one year almost to the day.

Sirens scream closer. A few seconds later, a patrol car screeches to a stop on the road. An officer hops out and hurries down the embankment and through the field toward Jimmy with one hand on his gun. His uniform is starched-stiff and shiny. His hair buzzed close to his scalp, looking like he's arrived straight from his academy graduation. He doesn't watch where he puts his feet, and before Jimmy can warn him, he slams his heavy-duty boot down on the bouquet, grinding the dried flowers into the mud.

The first cop to arrive on the scene, and this apple fritter, whose entire job is to preserve the evidence, is stepping on it instead. Obviously not the top of his class.

"You might want to watch where you put your feet." Jimmy points to the mess of wildflowers under his boot.

The hulking bull of a man, with dumb blinking cow eyes to match, lifts his foot and peers at the discarded bouquet. Maybe he really is as new as he looks. Maybe this is his first time responding to a report of a dead body. So maybe Jimmy shouldn't be too hard on him because everybody makes mistakes, and this one is an easy one to make considering they're standing near a field of plants identical to the ones in the bouquet. But then, the cop puts his foot back down in the exact same spot.

The bouquet sinks deeper into the mud.

"Are you the one who found the body?" His eyes roam over Jimmy's outfit. Slacks and loafers, the button-up checkered shirt with one-too-many pens sticking from the pocket. Not the best clothes for cutting through fields and exploring tangled woods in the dead heat of summer, but it was what he was wearing when the call came over the scanner, and he didn't have a chance to change before he left.

"I'm a reporter with the *Statesman Journal*." Jimmy flashes his press badge, then crouches and aims his camera at the bouquet and the standard-issue boot squashing it flat.

The click sounds as loud as a gunshot in the empty field.

"No pictures, buddy. I don't care who you work for." The cop lurches toward Jimmy and waves his hands in the air, like he's shooing away a stray cat.

He's about a foot taller than Jimmy and twice as thick through the chest and could probably lift Jimmy right off his feet and carry him out of here without any problem if he wasn't too lazy to try. Jimmy straightens and jabs his finger at the name tag stitched onto the man's uniform. Clodfelter. How appropriate.

"Mind if I call you Clod?" he asks.

"Name's Fred," the cop says, his mouth twisting and color rising in his cheeks. "But you can call me Officer."

"Sure thing, Officer. Now, you might want to bag up that evidence before your boss gets here and realizes you stepped all over it." Jimmy lifts the camera again, taking another picture, this time without Clodfelter's boot in the way.

Clodfelter sputters and reaches to grab Jimmy's elbow, but

Jimmy pulls away from him. "I wouldn't, if I were you. Freedom of the press and all that."

He waves his badge as he follows the creek into the trees.

Clodfelter seems torn about whether to chase after Jimmy or take care of the bouquet. Ultimately he decides on neither. He walks back across the field to where his police cruiser is parked at an angle on the gravel shoulder. There he rummages in the trunk for a few minutes before pulling out a spool of yellow tape and fumbling to loop it through two crooked fence posts edging the road.

Jimmy stops paying attention to the officer then. Clodfelter's got a checklist in his head of what needs to get done, and he's going to do it in that order whether or not it makes sense. This is Jimmy's chance to see the crime scene before anyone else, before more experienced officers show up and drag him back to the road. This is his chance to finally start putting the pieces together.

The dispatcher didn't give exact details of where to find the body, only that it was somewhere inside a cluster of trees near Crocker Creek. If she's anything like the others, Jimmy knows he'll find her close to the water.

A few steps later, he sees her exactly where he thought she'd be. Posed on her back at the edge of the creek. Like the others, she's naked. One arm folds across her chest, her fingers still clenched around the shape of flower stems. The other arm floats weightless in the water, which explains how the bouquet ended up separated from the body this time. Leaves and flowers similar to the ones found in the bouquet tangle in her long, blond hair spread like a fan around the crown of her head. Bruises darken her throat. Scratches cover her arms and legs.

Jimmy raises his face to the canopy and whispers an apology. Then he lifts his camera and begins to capture as many details as he can.

Every shadow and scuff, every fallen petal and bent stem. Every bruise, every scratch, every missing piece. Her wide, unseeing eyes. Her mottled flesh and the marks around her neck. Her pale skin streaked in mud. The maggots that wriggle in open wounds. The flies that give off an angry buzz as Jimmy bends close to her partially open mouth. If he were to jam a stick between her teeth and pry open her stiff jaw, he's pretty sure he would find her tongue cut out. But he doesn't touch her. He takes more pictures and swallows down rising nausea from the cloying stench of bog water and rot.

A branch snaps. Clodfelter appears in the woods behind him.

"You're not supposed to touch anything." He's trying to sound tough, but his trembling voice gives him away.

Clodfelter stands with a roll of yellow tape in one hand and a single high-top sneaker with orange laces in the other. He stares at the body. All the color drains from his cheeks, leaving his skin as pale as the burned-out August sky.

"You're not supposed to touch anything either." Jimmy gestures to the shoe.

The officer looks at it like he doesn't know how it got there. He drops it onto the ground and backs away. The sneaker looks too big to belong to the dead girl, but that's not the point. The point is that it's here, and so is she, and now Clodfelter's had his paws all over another piece of evidence. What's the purpose of calling the police if they're going to be this bad at their job?

"First time you've seen a dead body?" Jimmy asks.

Clodfelter turns, takes three steps to the side, and vomits into a patch of ferns.

Chapter 2

Within the hour, the fields and woods surrounding Crocker Creek are crawling with uniformed officers. Officer Clodfelter leans against the trunk of his car, his head hanging between his knees. Jimmy waits beside him, watching the methodical way the other men work over the field, wishing he could be out there with them, one more pair of eyes searching for some clue to point them in the right direction. He doesn't want this girl to end up like the others. Shoved into a box, forgotten.

An unmarked car pulls up behind the other cruisers parked along the side of the road, and a man dressed in a brown suit and red tie climbs out. *About damn time,* Jimmy thinks. The detective doesn't seem to be in a hurry, though. He takes a second to adjust his belt as he watches the activity through mirrored sunglasses. Then he pulls a cigarette and lighter from his pocket and lights up, inhaling deeply with the first hit.

Detective Michael Rausch is a man teetering between young and old, short and tall, solid and soft. Even his hair can't seem to decide. He's bald across the dome of his scalp, but thick, curly brown hair continues to grow along the sides and back. Jimmy has crossed paths with Rausch several times over the past six years.

You work the same beat long enough and show up to enough crime scenes, and the department becomes like a second family. And Michael Rausch is like the obnoxious, drunk uncle you leave the room to avoid. The amount of respect Jimmy has for the man couldn't even fill a shot glass, but victims don't get to pick who investigates their cases. There's a rotation, and, today, Michael Rausch is on deck.

He finishes his cigarette, drops the butt in the gravel, and walks over to where Jimmy and Clodfelter are standing.

"Helluva first day, Freddie boy." He slaps Clodfelter on the shoulder then turns his gaze onto Jimmy. "Don't tell me you're the one who called it in?"

Jimmy shakes his head. "Heard it over the scanner. I got here at the same time as Officer Clodfelter."

"No, you were here before me," Clodfelter says, his voice still thin and trembling.

Rausch's bushy eyebrows dart up, and he shakes his head. "If anyone else asks, Freddie boy, you were here first."

"But—" Clodfelter starts to protest.

Rausch ignores him and turns his attention to Jimmy instead.

"Walk with me." He claps his hand on Jimmy's shoulder and steers him toward the ditch. "I don't like reporters very much. But keep your enemies closer, I suppose, so why don't you start by talking me through everything you did when you got here. Everything you saw. Everything you touched. Everything you took pictures of."

He points at the camera Jimmy is still carrying in one hand.

Jimmy tells him everything, including how Clodfelter trampled the evidence. Even though he doesn't like Rausch, Rausch is all the hope this dead girl has. Rausch is the one who will decide how this case is handled, whether it's given priority or shuffled to the bottom of an ever-growing stack. He is the person who will determine if this girl will get the justice she deserves, or if, like the first three, she'll be ignored, her life reduced to two pitiful lines in a half-hearted press release:

> *An unidentified woman was found strangled and dumped near Crocker Creek. If you have any information regarding this event, please contact Salem Police.*

"I didn't get close enough to see," Jimmy says. "But once the coroner gets here, have him take a look inside her mouth. I have a feeling her tongue will be cut out like the others."

"What others?"

Jimmy remembers the first dead girl like it was yesterday. The summer of 1976 saw more rainfall than usual, turning the August days muggy and his skin slick with sweat. He'd been working the crime beat for the *Statesman Journal* for nearly three years at that point, and though he'd seen plenty of dead bodies in that short time, he'd never seen one that made him feel quite like this. Crushed and, at the same time, angry as hell.

He wanted to punch someone. He wanted to cry. He wanted to find the man who'd hurt this girl and tear him apart. He wanted to cover her nakedness and carry her off to some quiet place, far away from the black-booted asshats stomping through the trees where she'd been found.

The officers searching for evidence made jokes as they worked over the scene. They called her names. They treated her like a doll, a meat sack, a nothing. Jimmy knew part of their disconnection was protection against the horror of it. He could have respected that if they had worked half as hard at finding her killer as they had at cracking jokes.

The detective assigned to the first dead girl in 1976 was not the same detective assigned to the second dead girl in 1977 or the third one a year later. A different detective for every case and no wonder Rausch has no idea what Jimmy's talking about.

"Three girls in the past three years. All found in the middle of August. All found naked and arranged near the water, holding flowers. All three of them had their tongues cut out." Jimmy points toward the stand of trees where officers weave like shadow creatures through the trunks. "I think she might be the fourth."

They're halfway across the field when Rausch stops walking. Setting his hands on his hips and widening his stance, he turns to face Jimmy. "News to me. I haven't heard a damn thing about these other three. Why do you suppose that is?"

The first dead girl was never identified. She had a name, of course she did, but no one ever found out what it was. Her fingerprints weren't on file. By the time her body was found, decomposition, hastened by that summer's unusual amounts of rain, had turned her nearly unrecognizable. The list of missing girls in Oregon was long but proved useless. None of the girls on the list had two gold-capped molars on the left side of her lower jaw.

The second dead girl ended up as nameless and forgotten as the first, except it took a little longer to get there. Lucky her, she was found before decomposition had a chance to destroy her features. When the cops took a picture of her face around to local bars, one man said he knew her, said she was a hooker who gave five-dollar blow jobs. He said the woman called herself Dotty but that she hadn't given him a last name. And why would she? And who cares? After a half-hearted effort by the cops to uncover more information about Dotty, if that was even her real name, and getting no help from the other women like Dotty who might have known something, they shoved the file in a box and shoved that box in the back of the evidence room and never thought about her again.

The third dead girl was another sex worker, known to the police only as Maria. She'd been stopped several times in the months before her death, warned about soliciting, then sent on her way again. Jimmy remembers how the detective handling the case didn't even try to find out her last name, or where she came from, or if she had a family who might be wondering where their daughter had gone. When Jimmy asked, the detective shrugged his shoulders and asked, "What did she expect would happen?"

Jimmy did his best to write an article his editor, Tadd Crosby, would print on the front-page. These girls had family somewhere, someone who loved and missed them and would want to know what had happened in the end. He worried, too, about other young women working the streets, climbing into strangers' cars, driving to dark and secluded areas, every night wondering if this would be the night they didn't make it home alive. Jimmy thought if he could warn people about a possible serial murderer preying on vulnerable women, maybe he could keep it from happening again.

It took Tadd all of fifteen seconds to scan Jimmy's article before he crumpled it up and tossed it in the trash can beside his desk. "No one cares about dead girls who don't have names, Jimmy," he said, cracking his knuckles. "And no one cares about dead prostitutes either."

Jimmy went back to writing about burglaries and drug busts and a mother of three who went missing while on a trip to the Oregon Coast, but always in the back of his mind were the three dead girls no one else cared about.

Now it's August again, and there's a fourth body, and Jimmy is kicking himself for not pushing harder to tell the dead girls' stories when he had a chance. If he'd insisted the article went to print, maybe this new girl would still be alive.

"It's just a theory," Jimmy says to Rausch. "But yes, I think if you went back and took a look at those old files, you'd find similarities too striking to be a coincidence. And as for why you haven't heard about them? I don't know. Maybe you haven't been paying attention."

Rausch sputters a protest, but Jimmy ignores him and checks his watch. He promised his girlfriend, Melissa, that he'd meet her downtown for lunch. If he leaves now, he'll have time to swing by his apartment and change out of his sweat-drenched, dust-covered clothes, but then the coroner's silver van arrives. Two men pull a stretcher from the back and carry it through the field toward the trees.

Jimmy follows them, continuing to ignore Rausch, who's calling him a vulture and telling him to get lost. Jimmy's not going anywhere until this is done. Until he knows for sure. He stands close enough to see, but not close enough to be in the way, as the coroner kneels and reaches to open the dead girl's mouth.

Chapter 3

"You're late." Melissa sits stiffly at the diner's lunch counter with her eyes fixed on a television in the corner that's tuned to a local news station.

Jimmy leans in to kiss her cheek.

"And you stink." She finally turns to look at him, her dark brown eyes roaming over his windswept hair, the grass seeds clinging to his jacket, the dusty pant cuffs, and muddy boots. "You're filthy. Where have you been?" But before he can answer, she holds up her hand. "Don't tell me. You were working on a big story that couldn't possibly wait until later."

He's been dating Melissa since the end of February, but even in these six short months, he's been late for their dates more than he's been on time. And he's never once been early. She thought it was interesting at first. How he swept in at the last second with some harried and gruesome explanation for where he'd been. Ten car pile-up on the freeway. Bomb threat at the Capitol building. Suicide jumper off the Union Street Bridge. For a few weeks, she was in awe of him, of what he did and the words he wrote. Once, after spending the night at his place, she dragged the morning newspaper into bed and, naked and dappled in pink sunrise, read aloud an article he'd written about a double homicide. When she was finished, she gave a little shiver and asked him how he did it? How could he be around all that death and tragedy and not become tragic himself?

Without thinking, he said the first thing that came to mind. *You get used to it after a while.*

It wasn't the whole truth, but it was a lot of it.

She gave him a strange look after he said it. Her pert nose crinkled. Her smooth forehead folded into worried lines, and her full lips dragged into a pinched frown. He thinks this was when she realized he was no comic book hero, just a regular man doing a job that needed to be done. A job he was good at, by the way, and one he enjoyed most of the time despite the painful realities of meeting people on the worst days of their lives. He thinks this was when she decided to leave him.

She pretended for a few more weeks, then five days ago, she called him an ambulance chaser. *Isn't there anyone else who can write those horrible stories? Why don't you write about something nice once in a while? Something that doesn't end in someone dying.*

He knew it was over between them as soon as the words came out of her mouth. He doesn't want to be with someone who doesn't understand that his work is important to him and to the community he serves. He doesn't need this kind of contempt, but some cruel part of him clings to hope that she will change her mind and decide his work doesn't bother her that much after all. He's turning thirty in a few weeks, and he's tired of being alone on his birthday. He's tired of being alone. Period.

Besides that, he likes Melissa. He really does. She's smart. She works as a receptionist for one of the state senators, though Jimmy can never remember which one. She snorts a little when she laughs, and she laughs a lot. She is a bright spot in his dark days and always buys the beer he likes and reads books about plants so that when they go on walks, she's able to identify the flowers and weeds and trees and bushes. She likes orange cats and big dogs. She spent a summer in France and even still speaks the language a little.

Jimmy was starting to imagine a future with her. He introduced her to his mother. Maybe that's when the trouble started. Maybe it has nothing to do with his work. Maybe he rushed things, and that's when she started to pull away.

The reason doesn't matter now. She's leaving, and there's nothing Jimmy can do to stop her.

He slides onto the barstool next to Melissa and points at the empty wine glass near her elbow. "What are you drinking?"

"Is that your apology?"

"Come on, I was only ten minutes late."

"Thirteen minutes, according to my watch."

"Don't get upset."

"I'll get upset if I want to," she says. "The very least you could have done was call me so I didn't end up sitting here like an idiot wondering if I should order or not."

"Tony doesn't mind the company. Do you, Tony?" Jimmy smiles at the server who's here every weekday for the lunch rush.

The man's a couple decades older than Jimmy, and though he's never asked, Jimmy's pretty sure Tony owns the place. Tony shakes his head like he doesn't want to get involved and turns his attention to the television that's playing footage of Crocker Creek from earlier this morning.

The video was taken after the coroner arrived but before they removed the body. The field is dotted with officers. The television news crews hang back, staying on the road behind the yellow tape Clodfelter finally managed to set up properly.

"I couldn't call, Mel." Jimmy points at the television. "I was out there. And there aren't any phones that far out of town."

Melissa frowns at the screen. "You know I don't like that nickname."

This is news to him. She's never complained when he's called her Mel before. He decides this is another nail in their coffin. He reaches for her hand anyway because he has never been the one to quit on anything, even when he knows it's hopeless.

"I'm sorry, Melissa. I really am. I had every intention of being here on time. Of course I didn't want you to be sitting here waiting for me, but they found another girl."

He told her about the first three a couple of weeks ago after he accidentally fell asleep at her place. He usually didn't spend the night because her roommates, two other single women in their twenties, wouldn't approve, but he'd been up late the night before, trying to meet a tight deadline. Melissa's queen bed was so much softer than his lonely twin, and her sheets smelled of lavender. He couldn't help it. He fell asleep fast and hard. The next thing he knew, he was screaming himself awake, and Melissa was there rubbing his back, telling him everything was going to be all right. It was a nightmare, that was all, nothing to worry about.

She asked him what he'd been dreaming about, what he remembered. A girl screaming in the distance. Jimmy trying to get to her, running, but his legs get stuck in quicksand or break into a thousand pieces. The screaming grows louder, but no matter how fast he runs, Jimmy finds himself farther away. He knows he won't reach her in time, but still, he tries. Then the screaming stops.

It wasn't the first time he had a dream like this. He knows it won't be the last. In the quiet dark and soothing warmth of Melissa's lavender-scented sheets, Jimmy told her about the girls with no tongues and no names, the girls who haunt him now because there is no one else who cares as much as he does.

Melissa pulls her hand from Jimmy's grasp and slides off the vinyl stool.

He stands, too, reaching for his wallet to pay Tony for the wine and inconvenience, but Melissa waves him off. "Don't bother walking me out. We're done, Jimmy. I'm tired of playing mistress to your dead girls."

She fumbles in her purse a moment, pulls out a crumpled five-dollar bill, tosses it on the counter, and leaves. Her heels click across the worn linoleum floor.

Jimmy sinks back down onto the stool and orders pastrami and Swiss on rye.

Tony grunts like he thinks Jimmy's an idiot for letting Melissa storm off like that. Maybe he's right, but Jimmy can't be with a woman who's going to get upset every time he chooses a story over her.

Reporting is more than a job. It's in his blood. He'd do this work even if he didn't get paid. Because it's exciting. Because when he finds that missing piece and it starts to click together, he feels invincible. There's power in weaving a narrative, a deep satisfaction in telling stories that would otherwise be ignored, in giving voice to the voiceless.

———

Jimmy Eagan didn't always want to be a reporter.

Like most boys growing up, he dreamed about being a firefighter or a pilot or a heart surgeon or the President of the United States. He wanted to save lives and be the Grand Marshall of his hometown parade. He wanted the other boys in his class to envy him and the girls to blush when he walked past. But he was a scrawny kid with a wheezing chest, allergic to everything the same as his mother, with a bad case of acne and a tendency to stammer whenever the teacher called on him. The boys tripped him and called him names. The girls treated him like he didn't even exist.

Books became his refuge. Jimmy spent most of his junior high years hiding in the library, reading Jules Vern and Isaac Asimov, Patricia Highsmith and Ed McBain. He read history books, too. The rise and fall of the Roman Empire, the legacy of the English monarchy, the trenches of WWI, the horrors of WWII—he read anything and everything he could get his hands on until the librarian told him he'd go blind reading so much. But he was happy with books. They never expected anything of him. They never called him names. They existed for him, but also, he felt in many ways that he existed for them.

He joined the high school newspaper his freshman year on a whim because he needed extracurricular credits. He had been reading about Ambrose Bierce, a journalist who disappeared while investigating a story in Mexico, and thought that kind of life could be an exciting one. Traveling around the world, chasing stories and adventure—minus the disappearing part. He might not be able to save lives, but perhaps he could write about people who did.

It turned out writing suited him. He enjoyed it in the same way he enjoyed reading, in that it filled out the spaces of himself. Over time, he found he could write his way into existence. People who didn't know him at all would read his stories, and suddenly he was walking down the school hallways, listening to them talk about his front-page story. That was when he realized he could throw his words into the air and people would catch them and, if for a passing moment, he could feel known.

He worked hard and became his high school's youngest editor. Later, he applied and was accepted to Harvard, and even though his mother cried when he told her he was moving from Oregon to Massachusetts, her eyes glinted with pride.

Two days before Jimmy was set to leave, Betsy Eagan took her son out to his favorite shrimp and steak restaurant. While they waited for their meals to come, she said, "Your father was a writer, you know."

Betsy Eagan didn't talk much about Jimmy's father. The only thing Jimmy knew about the man was that his name was Walter, and he'd died three months before Jimmy was born. There were no pictures of him anywhere in the house, and the one time Jimmy asked about his father, Betsy had locked herself in her room for two whole days. Jimmy never spoke his father's name again.

When he was alone, he made up stories about how his father had died. Walter Eagan was an investment banker who got hit by a bus as he crossed a busy street. Walter Eagan was a cowboy who was gored by a bull in a rodeo show. Walter Eagan died saving someone's life. Now, over a plate of buttered shrimp and medium-rare steak, his mother told him that Walter Eagan was none of those things. Walter Eagan was a writer, a newspaperman just like Jimmy was going to be. He was also a poet.

"Oh, he wrote me the most beautiful poems." Betsy smiled the coyest of smiles, and Jimmy knew that no one would ever read those poems but her.

"Is that how he died?" Jimmy asked. "Was he investigating a story?"

He was thinking again of Ambrose Bierce, of how one theory claimed Bierce had been shot to death by a firing squad after accusations of being a traitor and spy.

Betsy's smile sloped to a frown, and her eyes darted around the restaurant in a way that made Jimmy think his father's death was a state secret. So maybe his father stumbled upon a political scandal, a CIA investigation gone wrong, the truth about Area 51.

But no, his mother said, no, it was nothing as grand as all that. Walter Eagan was stabbed in a dark alley when he was walking home from work, mugged over the ten dollars he had in his wallet and the fake gold watch he wore on his wrist. By the time someone found him, he'd already bled out, and there was nothing to be done but send someone to tell his six-month pregnant wife to start planning a funeral.

Jimmy pushed his surf-and-turf around on his plate, unable to eat any more.

His mother reached across the table and brushed her warm fingers across his cheek. "You look just like him. You have his eyes."

A deep blue, the bluest of blues, so blue they were almost black. The kind of eyes that noticed everything, even what other people missed. Like how the man at the table next to them was wearing two different colored socks and unpolished shoes; and how the server had a scar behind her left ear, only visible when she tilted her head a certain way; and how the woman near the door kept twisting her wedding ring and biting her lip, so nervous about something that when a man arrived with a bouquet of roses, Jimmy was pretty sure he wasn't the woman's husband.

"He would be so proud of you," Betsy said, lifting her hand to ask for the check.

Jimmy grabbed the bill before his mother could. It was the first time he paid for dinner like that, like a grown man. His mother blushed and beamed and dabbed a single tear from the corner of her eye. And it was there, as Jimmy was counting out the correct dollars and change, that he realized he hadn't simply stumbled into journalism. Without knowing it, his entire life, he'd been following in his father's footsteps. He was always going to end up a writer.

Stories were his legacy, and now they were his destiny, too. It was on that day, walking across the restaurant parking lot, a fine mist glittering on the windshield, that Jimmy made a promise to himself and to the memory of his father. He would carry on the tradition, live the life Walter Eagan had barely started. He would uncover secrets, seek out truths, expose the lies. He would write stories that mattered. He would make his father proud.

Tony brings Jimmy the pastrami and Swiss on rye, sets it on the counter, and asks if he wants anything else.

"Bring me whatever's on tap," Jimmy says.

It's barely noon, but the way this day has been, it feels closer to five o'clock.

While Tony fills a pint, Jimmy takes a notebook and pen from his messenger bag, flips to an empty page in the middle, and writes down everything he knows about girl number four, which admittedly isn't much.

There was nothing in that field to help identify her, and Jimmy can only hope this time someone is looking for her, someone who will step forward and claim her as their own. Otherwise, she'll end up as forgotten as the others.

Before leaving the scene, Jimmy gave Detective Rausch his business card.

"You'll call me if you ID her?" Jimmy asked.

Rausch gave him a look like calling Jimmy was the last thing he would ever do but tucked the business card in his pocket anyway.

Beer spills over the edge of the glass when Tony sets it down on the counter. Jimmy wipes it up with a napkin. On the television screen, Detective Rausch talks to a reporter. He confirms that a homicide is being investigated, but says there is no danger to the public at this time.

Jimmy snorts.

Tony shoots a glance over to him. "They lying about that?"

"You got a daughter, Tony?"

Tony shakes his head. "Two boys."

"Then I'd say you've got nothing to worry about." Jimmy reaches for his beer.

CHAPTER 4

It's late afternoon when Jimmy gets back to the *Statesman Journal* offices. He shoves aside his disappointment over Melissa as he sits down at his desk to type out an article describing his morning at Crocker Creek. Each letter is a hammer strike inside his temple, the typewriter a soundtrack to his anger. There should have never been a fourth girl. If the police did their job from the beginning. If the public bothered to pay any attention. If his editor cared about more than just the bottom line.

The door to his editor's office swings open at that moment, and Thaddeus Crosby III, Tadd to those who know him, pops his head out. Tadd is a middle-aged man with a full head of jet-black hair that sticks out in all directions because he's in the habit of tugging on it anytime he's trying to concentrate. A five o'clock scruff darkens his square chin. He scans the press room, then points a finger at Jimmy. "What do you got for me?"

"A woman's body was found near Crocker Creek."

A frown teases the corners of Tadd's mouth. "Got a name?"

"Not yet."

"Get me a name, or the story's not worth anyone's time." Tadd turns to go back into his office.

"I think she's another August girl," Jimmy says, trying to hold his editor's attention.

Tadd pauses with his hand on the door. "You're going down this rabbit hole again?"

"It's not a rabbit hole, Tadd. Three women, now four, all strangled, all left near streams, holding bouquets of wildflowers."

"And?"

"They've all had their tongues cut out. That's more than a simple coincidence."

"Are the police connecting the cases yet?"

Jimmy knows he's lost the argument, but he tries anyway. "They aren't paying attention. But I am, and I know exactly what I'm looking at here. We've got another serial murderer preying on young women, and if we don't start warning the public—"

"Do you know why Ted Bundy is so interesting?" Tadd asks, interrupting him. "Why the public can't seem to get enough?"

In 1976, Bundy was convicted of aggravated kidnapping and later charged with the murder of a nurse in Colorado. He escaped from prison before he could stand trial. One year after his escape, he was arrested again in Florida and charged with the murder of two college students. On July 24, 1979, after a month-long trial in Miami, Bundy was convicted and sentenced to death row.

His trial was the first to be nationally televised. Like most of the nation, and any crime reporter with half a brain, Jimmy has been following Ted Bundy's story closely. He's a different kind of killer, horrifying in his relatability. Handsome and charismatic, educated and organized. His crimes, multiple arrests, escapes, and subsequent trials have turned him into a sensation. People love to hate him. Some women simply love him, despite, or perhaps because of his violence. Ever since his conviction three weeks ago, Ted Bundy has been all anyone wants to talk about. Put his name in bold and a picture of his charismatic smile on the front-page and papers fly off the rack.

Tadd doesn't wait for Jimmy's answer. "It's because he's handsome, sure. Everyone likes a good-looking villain. But it's also because he killed promising young women, girls who were beloved, cherished, missed. As awful as it may be, it's how this business works. We sell more papers when people are afraid they could be the next one killed. If your man, if he even exists, if he's just killing prostitutes, then what do the rest of us have to worry about?"

Jimmy cringes at his editor's callous dismissal of the victims. He hasn't been working in the newspaper business nearly as long as Tadd, but he understands that certain stories hook readers faster than others. Demographics come into play, so does relatability. What he doesn't understand, what he may never understand, is how virtue, or the lack of it, determines whose life is worth writing about and whose gets discarded.

Tadd sighs and shakes his head. "Look, I know this story's important to you, so how about a compromise? Do you know what the *New York Post* is calling Bundy now? The Love-Bite Killer. If you can't dig up a name for the girl, then at least come up with a clever moniker for your killer. If you can do that, I'll make sure your story's on the front-page tomorrow."

Jimmy nods. "Gimme ten minutes."

"Bring it to me in five." Tadd steps into his office and slams the door shut.

Jimmy bends over the typewriter again.

Ted Bundy didn't kill the August girls, but it isn't a stretch to imagine someone with a similar vile nature. Another man who hates women, who blends in and changes his appearance to appear harmless. Another chameleon who would be hard to track down, harder still because, right now, no one but Jimmy is looking for him. But maybe Tadd's right. Maybe what people need is something to sink their teeth into, a monster to hunt down with pitchforks and flames.

Jimmy can do that. If it means more people paying attention and demanding action from the police, he'll play the game the way Tadd wants it to be played. He'll give this devil a name.

———

Jimmy Eagan stumbled into the crime beat after the man assigned before him quit without notice on Jimmy's first day at the *Statesman Journal*. He didn't have a press badge yet, didn't even know which desk he'd be working at. He was still wearing his rain jacket, standing in the middle of the press room, feeling a bit baffled by all the commotion, when a man with a red pen tucked behind his ear, and another tucked in the pocket of his striped shirt, grabbed his elbow.

"You better be our new cubbie." These were the first words Tadd ever said to Jimmy, and Jimmy, newly graduated from Harvard with a Master's Degree in English, squeaky with bright-eyed idealism, nodded, eager to get started on whatever story his new editor assigned.

"I'm looking forward to—"

But Tadd cut him off. "You're younger than I thought you'd be."

Jimmy heard that a lot. He was twenty-four but barely looked a day over eighteen. After graduation, he'd spent three months in Europe touring art museums, eating too much food, and trying to grow a beard. The chin hair grew in patchy and clearly did nothing to make him look older. He would give it two more weeks before he shaved it off again.

Tadd laughed and cuffed his shoulder. "No, that's good, that's good. Young means I can teach you how to do this job right from the beginning, unlike these other dummies who can't tell their gerunds from their assholes. Now. Tell me, kid. Have you ever covered the crime beat before?"

There hadn't been enough crime at Harvard to merit a designated reporter. Even if there had been, Jimmy wouldn't have wanted the assignment. Crime was base. Crime was people living through their worst moments. Jimmy didn't want to write about that. He wanted to write about people changing the course of the world, fighting the good fight, and living their best moments. When he returned to Oregon after six years in academia and accepted the position with the *Statesman Journal*, he imagined himself starting small with local politics.

Salem was the Oregon State Capitol. There would be plenty of stories to cover. He pictured himself walking into that marble-domed rotunda in a suit and tie, asking hard-hitting questions, making sure the politicians answered to the people. Eventually, after gaining experience on the state level, he would start reporting on international matters. Wars and peace talks, trade deals, the UN, anything and everything that had to do with the flux and flow of world politics. Crime was not something he ever considered. It was not something he understood enough to write about.

"It doesn't matter." Tadd dragged Jimmy into his office and handed him a press badge with someone else's name on it. "You're my crime guy now. You know where the Capitol Street Bank is? Get Ava to draw you a map on the way out. Some idiots tried to rob a bank, and it ended in a shoot-out. A couple of cops got injured. I need you down there five minutes ago to find out what the hell is going on and who the hell's responsible. Get it right, and you might even get your first front-page story in the morning. Think you can handle that?"

Five hours later, running on three cups of coffee and adrenaline, Jimmy turned in his first piece as a crime reporter for the *Statesman Journal*. He felt immensely proud when he set the two-page article on Tadd's desk. Even prouder when Tadd slashed red pen through half of it and told him to write it up again, but shorter. Another hour and finally, he was ready to go home, but Tadd stopped him on his way out the door. He shoved what looked like a handheld radio transceiver at Jimmy.

"It's a portable scanner," Tadd explained. "It's already programmed to the stations the police use. You listen to their chatter. Anything sounds interesting, you jump in your car and go get the story. Questions?"

Jimmy took the scanner and tucked it into the pocket of his messenger bag.

"That's your new best friend," Tadd said. "It's on whenever you're awake. Take it with you wherever you go. Always carry a spare battery." He laughed and thumped Jimmy on the back. "Don't look so scared, kid. As long as you deliver the goods and stay on top of your deadlines, you'll get along just fine here."

It took Jimmy six weeks to learn the scanner.

At first, he leaped into action every time the dispatcher's voice broke through the static to call out a code. He didn't understand the strings of numbers and letters, but the dispatcher always gave an address or cross-street. So he scratched that part on a piece of paper, jumped in his car, and headed to the scene. He got lost a lot those first few weeks and often showed up after the cops had already come and gone. But a few times, he got lucky and arrived on scene at the same time as the responding officers. When that happened, he felt a rush of adrenaline as he stepped out of the car. But rarely was it anything interesting. Windows smashed, kids tagging a wall, a drunk man wandering into the middle of the street. Once there was a fight outside a bar, but the cops broke it up quickly and sent both men home with a warning.

When he brought the stories to his editor, Tadd would read the first few lines, then tear the paper in half and throw it in the trash.

"I don't care about any of this stuff, and neither do our readers. Do you know what kinds of stories sell papers, Jim-boy?" He didn't wait for an answer. "Murder, political scandals, anything that has to do with sex. And do you know what all those things have in common? People. No one cares about broken windows and vandalized fences. People want to read about people."

Tadd was a good editor. Tough but patient. He knew Jimmy was still new to the work, still trying to figure it out. "But you'd better figure it out quicker than this," he said after the second week of bad articles. "You've got one week to bring me something more interesting than kids throwing beer bottles off the overpass, or else."

Tadd didn't say what the 'or else' would be, but Jimmy had a pretty good idea. If he wasn't contributing, then he was dead weight, and dead weight got cut.

So Jimmy started to listen for keywords. Shots fired, suspect on the run, possible dead body, respond with sirens. Anytime the police needed to rush to a scene with lights and sirens blaring, the odds were high that someone's life was probably in danger.

Tadd started reading Jimmy's articles all the way through to the end. Then he started editing them from five paragraphs down to three lines. "This is good content, Jim-boy. This is the kind of stuff I'm talking about, but we don't need all this extra fluff. Tell the people how many bodies and if those bodies were famous. Tease them, keep them coming back for more."

As Jimmy became more familiar with the scanner's jargon, he realized he could tune out most of it and respond only to the codes he knew would bring him a good story.

He no longer startles when the scanner crackles to life and the familiar voice of the dispatcher calls out a code. His heart no longer races at the thought of what might be coming next, if this will be it, his next big story. Usually, it isn't. Sometimes it is. But he can tell the difference now. When to go, when to stay, when to brace himself for the worst. The voices through the scanner are family now; the white noise crackling in the background has become the soundtrack to his dreams.

The scanner is sitting on the corner of his desk now, quiet, waiting. He types the final sentence in his article about the dead girl at Crocker Creek and tugs the paper from the typewriter, adding it to the stack to give to Tadd.

His eyes scan the paragraph where he describes how all four women were posed.

The first time he saw a photograph of the second victim, he was reminded of a painting he saw in one of the museums he visited when he was in Europe. A young woman floats on her back in a dark river. Her mouth is open, her hands lifted above the water's surface, offering a final prayer, or maybe she's giving someone the chance to grab hold and pull her to safety. Weeds and flowers tangle in her hair and fingers. The tragic drowning of Ophelia. The August girls may not have drowned, but their expressions in death were the same. Ruin, despair, the empty gaze of misspent hope.

THE OPHELIA KILLER STRIKES AGAIN.

Jimmy thinks Tadd will be happy with a headline like that. As he pushes his chair back, the desk phone beside his elbow rings. He answers, not letting it ring twice. "Jimmy here."

"Oh, good," the voice purrs. "I was hoping I'd catch you before you left."

"Hello, Annabeth. You're working late today."

Annabeth Falco has been working as a secretary for the Salem Police since Jimmy started this beat six years ago. From the beginning, Jimmy made sure that whenever he stopped in at the downtown precinct, he brought something for Annabeth. Never anything fancy. A muffin. A candy bar. A hot cup of coffee. He still brings her things and makes sure to compliment her hair, too, even if it's the same drab brown bun every time. It isn't bad hair, but it's nothing very special either. He tells her she looks nice. He smiles at her when he asks for favors. Says please and thank you. He treats her like a human being because he knows damn well that the men she works with treat her like a glorified copy machine. A little bit of human decency, that's all anyone asks for, and that little bit of decency, those simple things Jimmy does to make Annabeth feel seen, they've paid off for him. She's come to like him more than she likes the men she works with every day. So when something important happens at the precinct, Jimmy is the first person she calls.

"It's chaos down here," she says in a hushed whisper like she's got her hand cupped around the phone so no one else will hear.

There's commotion in the background, people shouting, then it gets quiet again, and in a breathless rush, Annabeth says, "She has a name, Jimmy. The woman we found at Crocker Creek this morning? We know who she is this time."

Chapter 5

The *Statesman Journal's* Thursday Edition lands on porch steps and driveways before sunrise the morning of August 16th. By breakfast, everyone in the greater Salem area knows about the Ophelia Killer and the name of his fourth victim.

Cherish Spalding was nineteen years old, a nursing student studying at Willamette University. Her father is a dentist. Her mother is a homemaker. She has a younger sister, Trina, and an Irish Setter named Chappy. She grew up in Portland. Her family still lives there. Her school of choice was far enough away for her to feel independent and still close enough to go home on the weekends if she needed to do laundry or missed Sunday dinners. She lived with two other girls in a rental house near campus. That's as much as Annabeth knew last night, as much as she was willing to tell Jimmy over the phone anyway. Out of respect for the family, he didn't put every detail into the article. He wrote enough to get people interested and to get them to feel something more than indifference.

It works.

Tadd grabs Jimmy as soon as he walks into the press room. "Your Ophelia Killer piece is blowing up, kid. It's big news. Huge.

The entire city's in a frenzy over this. You think you can get a follow-up piece written by deadline today?"

He nods. He already has half of it written.

According to Annabeth, the family was informed late last night about their daughter's death, but the police are waiting to hold a press conference until later today.

Jimmy won't be attending. He knows what they're going to say. Detective Rausch will ask for the public's help. He'll parade the grieving parents in front of the cameras. He'll say they aren't taking questions at this time. The whole thing will take less than ten minutes, and Rausch won't tell the gathered reporters anything Jimmy doesn't already know. It will be a waste of his time. Not to mention Rausch will want to know how he broke the story first, who gave him Cherish Spalding's name, and there's no way in hell Jimmy's throwing Annabeth under that bus. Not after everything she's done for him.

Instead, Jimmy grabs a cup of coffee from the breakroom and checks his messages in case there's new information about Cherish from Annabeth. There isn't, so he finishes his coffee and heads out again, driving to the address Annabeth gave him last night.

The house is a single-story rectangle with a garage on one side and concrete steps leading to the front door. Jimmy knocks. It takes a minute, but finally, the door cracks open. A young woman with frizzy blond hair, puffy eyes, and red-streaked cheeks peers out at him.

"You wouldn't happen to be Emily, would you? Or Tina?" He offers a close-lipped smile, wanting to put her at ease without coming across as a salesman. Annabeth told him the names of Cherish's roommates but didn't have details about what they look like.

"I'm Emily." The girl wipes her sleeve across her nose. "Who are you?"

He shows her his press badge. "I'm trying to find out what happened to Cherish."

Emily lets out a loud sob, then claps her hand over her mouth as if embarrassed to display such emotion. After a second, she opens the door wider and invites Jimmy inside.

As she leads him into a living room, where a brunette lies curled under an afghan on a couch that's sagging badly in the middle, Emily says, "Her dad called us last night. It still doesn't seem real. It can't be real."

The brunette sits up when they enter the room but keeps the blanket pulled tightly around her shoulders.

"Tina, this is Jimmy. He's here to talk to us about Cherish." Emily sinks onto the couch beside the brunette and tucks up her feet.

There aren't any lights on in the living room. A sliver of daylight shines through a narrow strip where the heavy velvet curtains don't quite meet in the middle. Both girls are pale, but the shadows in the room turn them a sickly gray. Their grief reeks of unwashed hair and Vicks VapoRub. Crumpled tissues litter the couch and carpet.

The brunette blinks up at Jimmy like she's blinking up at the sun. "Are you the police?"

"He's a reporter," Emily says.

Tina frowns. "I don't think we should talk to reporters."

"No one else is talking to us." Emily leans toward Jimmy, who's still standing in the middle of the room, trying to decide where to sit.

Besides the couch, there aren't many options. There's a Papasan chair covered in laundry, a fireplace hearth covered in dirty glasses and mugs, and an ottoman with a stack of textbooks piled on top. Jimmy decides to stay standing. He moves closer to the windows, pulling open the curtain a half an inch to let a little more light into the room.

"The police haven't come by to talk with you yet?" Jimmy asks.

"Mr. Spalding said they would, but you're the first person who's actually come," Emily says.

Detective Rausch will be too busy fielding calls from reporters and the mayor about Jimmy's article, how a serial murderer has been able to fly under the radar like this for so long. He'll be dealing with Cherish's parents, too, and trying to organize his team, dividing up who's going to do what. Rausch will send someone to interview Emily and Tina. Maybe he'll even come himself, but it won't be until tomorrow at the earliest, maybe even a few days from now.

"Do you know what happened?" Emily asks. "Mr. Spalding didn't tell us much. He said she was murdered, but that's all he said. Do you know who did it?"

"No, but that's what I'm trying to find out."

"You're helping the police?" Tina asks, chewing on the skin around her fingernail.

Jimmy nods. "And anything you can tell me about Cherish will be helping them, too."

"What do you want to know?" From Emily's expression, Jimmy can tell she's eager to contribute however she can.

But Tina's wary of him. "Emily," she says, touching her friend's knee. "Maybe we should wait and talk to an actual detective?"

"Do you want him to come back, Tina?" Emily's voice is shrill with panic. "Do you want him to kill us next?"

Tina withdraws and burrows deeper into the blanket. Her gaze lingers on the window to the left of where Jimmy is standing. Fear creeps in from the shadows edging the room.

Jimmy feels the shift, the sudden rise in tension.

"Was someone bothering Cherish?" he asks. "Someone you were worried about?"

The girls exchange a glance. Tina gives the slightest shake of her head, but Emily ignores her warning, gets up from the couch, and crosses to the window. She pulls the curtain all the way open and points across the street.

"We saw him a couple times standing under that street lamp.

Always at night. Always when Cherish was home. He would smoke cigarettes. We could see the embers burning red."

"Could you see his face? Can you describe what he looks like?"

Emily draws the curtain closed again and shakes her head. She returns to the couch. Tina offers her half of the blanket, and Emily tucks it around her lap.

"His face was always shadowed. Like, there's that street lamp, right?" Emily flicks her hand at the window. "But he would stand perfectly under it, so his hat made a shadow over his face."

"So he wore a hat?" Jimmy prods.

"A baseball cap, maybe?" Emily looks at Tina, who nods in agreement.

"What else did he wear?"

"Just a sweatshirt, pants. Everything was black."

"It wasn't a sweatshirt," Tina interjects. "It was a jacket, like a trench coat or something. He would keep his hands in his pockets, like here." She demonstrates, holding her hands down at her sides, close to the tops of her knees.

"Yeah, a long coat, that's it," Emily says.

But that's all they can really say about him. A man dressed head-to-toe in black lurking in the shadows in his long coat, smoking cigarettes. None of them approached him. They never thought to call the cops.

"We kind of hoped he'd get bored and go away," Emily says and starts crying again, this time doing nothing to stop the flood of tears. She leans into Tina's shoulder, and Tina wraps her arms around her.

"You should talk to Eric," Tina says, her voice taking on false bravado. "He and Cherish were hanging out a lot."

"They were dating?"

Tina shakes her head. "He probably had a crush on her, though."

Emily stops sniffling long enough to say, "Everyone had a crush on her."

"But she didn't like him like that," Tina adds. "She made it very clear they were just friends."

"And how did Eric feel about that?" Jimmy asks, knowing how closely feelings of love ran alongside feelings of rage. It didn't take much for a person to switch from one to the other.

"You think he could have killed her?" Emily stares wide-eyed at him.

"Do you?"

The girls exchange that secret glance again, silent words passing between them.

"No, absolutely not," says Tina.

"Eric's a nice guy," Emily adds.

"I'd like to talk to him all the same," Jimmy says. "Do you know where I can find him?"

According to the girls, Eric works weekend lunch shifts at a pizza joint near campus. Jimmy jots the name of the restaurant in his notebook.

He spends another hour with Tina and Emily, asking them about Cherish, about the kind of person she was, how she spent her days, what made her happy, what made her sad, who she dreamed of becoming. He asks to see Cherish's room. He doesn't touch anything, doesn't rummage, even though he wants to. It's one thing talking to the roommates before Detective Rausch gets a chance; it's another thing rifling through her belongings which may someday be gathered as evidence. The story Jimmy wants to tell isn't going to be found in her jewelry box or under the bed anyway. It's going to be found in the people who loved her, the people who would give anything to bring her back.

He thanks Tina and Emily, gives them his business card, and shows himself out. Before he gets in his car, he crosses the street to where Emily said the man would stand and watch. Jimmy scans the ground, hoping for cigarette butts or other evidence someone else was here, but there's nothing. From this spot, he can see straight into the girls' front window.

Chapter 6

Jimmy is the first customer inside Antonio's Pizza when it opens at noon on Friday. He takes one look at Eric Rhodes, reading a Wallace Stegner book behind the counter, and knows he's not the one who killed Cherish Spalding. He didn't kill any of the other three girls either.

He's young. Jimmy guesses him to be eighteen, nineteen, maybe. But he could just as easily be sixteen for how small he is—a skinny-limbed, concave-chested boy with a smooth, plump, milky-white face. The first girl turned up dead four years ago when Eric would have been all of fourteen. He looks like he can barely hold that two-hundred-page paperback for more than a few minutes, let alone subdue a terrified woman. No, Jimmy knows the second he walks into the pizza shop that Eric Rhodes is not his man.

But maybe he'll be able to tell Jimmy who is.

The kid is so lost in his book, he doesn't look up until Jimmy clears his throat and taps his fingers on the countertop. He leaps so high he almost falls off the stool. The book lands on the floor with a loud thump. Eric swoops to pick it up and mutters his apologies. He tugs on the apron tied around his waist, stretches a fake smile over his mouth, and says, "What can I get ya?"

"Slice of pepperoni," Jimmy says, "and a Coke."

"That'll be three dollars."

Jimmy slides money across the counter. "Your name's Eric, right?"

The button pinned to his chest tells him as much, but Jimmy asks anyway with a warm smile to break the ice. The kid nods, suspicious, as he puts the three dollars in the register. He crosses to where four already-made pizzas are waiting under warming lights, spatulas out a single slice, and puts it in the oven to reheat.

"You go to the university?" Jimmy asks.

Eric nods again but says nothing.

"Did you know that girl they found? Cherish Spalding?" Jimmy watches him carefully. You can tell a lot about a person by how they react to the name of a dead friend.

Eric's shoulders slump. He seems to go limp. His arms fall to his side and hang there a moment, and then a slight shudder rolls through him from head to toe, and he lifts his hands again to take the pizza from the oven before it burns. He slides it onto a paper plate and hands the plate to Jimmy. The slice glistens with grease.

"Yeah," he says, a wistful sadness in his voice. "Yeah, we had a couple of classes together. We're both in the nursing program."

He pours Coke into a paper cup, sets it on the counter, picks up his book, and sits back down on the stool to read.

Later, as Jimmy's eating his pizza, Eric comes over to his table. He's taken off his apron and holds it in one hand. He's on break, he says and asks if he can sit down. Jimmy gestures to the empty booth across from him.

"Why did you ask about Cherish?" Eric asks, eying the messenger bag sitting on the bench beside Jimmy. "Are you a reporter or something?"

"I am. Her roommates told me the two of you were friends. Maybe more than friends?"

Eric laughs, but it's a grief-filled sound. He glances at the clock hanging on the wall above the register. "I only have a few minutes."

But a few minutes is all Jimmy needs.

They talk about Cherish, how Eric met her during a freshman mixer for the nursing department. The entire room was filled with young women except for Eric. They whispered and giggled and gaped at him because men became doctors, didn't they? Feeling embarrassed and out of place, Eric was about to leave when he made eye contact with Cherish across the room. She smiled at him. A genuine smile. Then she waved him over and handed him a plastic cup filled with some kind of fruit punch. Instead of asking him why the hell he wanted to become a nurse—in that horrified tone everyone else used—she asked him about his favorite books and his favorite food. She asked if he had ever seen a dead body and then leaned in to whisper that after the party was over, she'd take him to where they kept the cadavers. She was part of a work-study program, and because it was her job to clean up the science buildings, she had keys that could get them inside the anatomy lab.

"She was nice to me," Eric says. "But we didn't like each other like that. Everyone thought we did, and whatever, we didn't care what everyone said. But, no, we were just friends." His cheeks flush red, and his gaze flicks down to the table. He rubs his thumb over a small crack in the Formica. "I don't...I'm not interested in girls like that."

Jimmy asks if Cherish told him about the man lurking outside the house or ever mentioned being afraid.

Eric shakes his head. "She wasn't afraid of anything. Not blood, not needles, not Professor Trenton, who'll flunk you for yawning during his class." He thinks a minute, then adds, "She had nightmares, though. She told me that once. She never said what they were about, just that sometimes she had trouble sleeping, so she'd get dressed and go walking at night, around her block as many times as it took her to feel tired again."

"Did she ever go farther than that? Did she ever walk out on the highway?"

Eric shrugs. "She might have, I don't know." The boy's brow furrows in thought, and he shakes his head like he disagrees with his own memories. "No, she wouldn't do something that dangerous. She would never be that stupid."

He sinks his head into his hands. "I can't believe she's dead. When Emily called me, I laughed. Then I got mad at her. She's always playing these pranks. And I thought that's what this was. But then I saw it on the news, too."

He moves his hands, cradling his stomach like he's going to be sick. "It's my fault."

"Why would you say that?"

"I told her I'd go to this party with her, but I backed out at the last minute. I had a paper due the next day, I couldn't."

"When was the party?"

"Sunday night. Some friends were meeting out at Minto Island. They were going to hang out and listen to music, I don't know." His cheeks pale. "That was the last time I talked to her. She called me a stick-in-the-mud."

Jimmy cranes his head to try and see behind the front counter. "Is anyone else working today, Eric?"

"Spencer's here. He's in the back."

"Maybe you should take the rest of the day off? Your friend just died. I'm sure your boss will understand."

"No." He shakes his head and sits up straighter. "No, I'm fine. This isn't the first time I've lost someone close to me. Work is a good distraction." His lip trembles, and he wipes the back of his hand across his dry cheeks. "It's funny, isn't it? The way the universe echoes?"

"What do you mean?"

"My big sister ran away from home when I was eleven." Eric's gaze drifts out the window. "Some hiker found her a week later. She'd been strangled and left to rot in the woods. Same as Cherish. I can't help but think that it has something to do with me." His brown eyes have taken on a haunted look when he turns back to Jimmy and asks, "Do you believe in curses?"

Jimmy drives straight to Eugene after leaving Eric to work the rest of his shift at Antonio's. It takes him about an hour to get to the *Register-Guard* newspaper offices, where he calls in a favor with a reporter he knows who writes features. Dexter Thomas is bug-eyed behind thick coke-bottle glasses, but even half-blind, he can see a good story brewing from miles away.

"What is it this time, Jimmy?" He has a whisper of a British accent. "Political scandal? Governor caught cheating on his wife? Shake up at the Capitol?"

"You know I'm on the crime beat."

Dexter rolls his eyes and huffs. "I thought you'd have sloughed off that albatross by now. Crime's a dead-end, Jimmy. You still working under that troglodyte Tadd? Let me talk to Paul and see if something is opening up here."

"I'm fine where I'm at, Dex. I just need your help digging up some old articles about a girl murdered in this area about ten years ago? Sometime in 1969? Hikers found her in McKinley Forest."

Dexter grimaces like he's bitten down on something sour, but he gestures for Jimmy to follow him toward the archive room. "Let's see what we can find, but I'm gonna need more information than that. You know how it is," he says with a shrug. "Dead girls are a dime a dozen."

Her name was Lydia Rhodes. She was barely eighteen, just two days past her birthday, and a recent graduate from North Eugene High School. She worked at a drive-thru burger joint and is survived by her parents and younger brother. The *Register-Guard* didn't turn her into a big enough story for Jimmy to get more details than this. Her killer was never found.

Jimmy drives across town to the central police precinct where, thanks to a call from Dexter, a detective waits for him in the lobby.

"We don't normally let just anyone come in and look at our cases like this," the middle-aged man with a slight paunch and severe crew cut says. "But Dex vouches for you, and around here, that's as good as gold. He says you might have some new leads for us, too."

He brings Jimmy into an interview room where a single cardboard box sits in the middle of the table. "You'll have to look at it all right here, of course. I can't have you taking any of it out of the station."

He pats the lid of a cardboard box. Dust puffs into the air.

"This is all there is?" Jimmy asks.

The detective shrugs and glances at his watch. "How long do you think you'll be? My shift ends soon."

"Are you the one working this case?" Jimmy takes the lid off the box and begins to flip through the documents.

"No one's working it," the detective says. "It's ten years old. If I remember right, the girl was initially reported as a runaway. There was no reason to suspect anything else had happened to her until her body turned up in those woods. Not much physical evidence to go off of, and all the leads we had turned out to be dead-ends anyway. There's not much else you can do when that happens but wait until someone comes forward with new information. The original investigator retired a few years ago. We just don't have the resources to actively work on cold cases like this one."

Jimmy flips through a stack of witness statements and written reports. He scans paragraph after paragraph, looking for similarities to Cherish and the other August girls. Halfway through the stack, he comes across a financial statement showing several withdrawals over the weeks leading up to Lydia's death but no deposits. The money in the Rhodes' checking account was hovering dangerously close to zero. In the margins, someone had written:

Broke. Dad was a drunk. Couldn't hold a job. Mom turning tricks in cheap hotel rooms on the weekend. Daughter doing the same?

Jimmy sets the document aside and moves on to the next, but he feels a tension headache coming on. A sharp spike of pain in his right temple flares as knots clench down the side of his neck.

Lydia Rhodes' story is all too familiar. Her life and death echoing years later with the three girls killed and dumped in Salem each August in 1976, 1977, and 1978. Poor girls, young girls, angry girls, girls at the end of their ropes, girls looking for a way out, looking for someone to take them out of their wretched lives. They had found someone, all right, someone who didn't give a damn about saving them.

But Cherish Spalding is different. From what Jimmy knows about her, she wasn't a girl on the edge, and she wasn't looking for a way out of anywhere. She had plans for her life and a bright future. She had resources, family, friends, ties with her community. She wasn't exactly the easiest of targets, and this gives Jimmy pause.

Maybe Lydia and the others aren't connected to Cherish at all, and maybe in his eagerness to link the cases, Jimmy's missing something important.

Then, at the very bottom of the box, he finds the autopsy report. Broken hyoid bone. Petechiae. Postmortem excision of the tongue, cut clean with the sharpest of blades. The Ophelia Killer might be changing the types of girls he hunts, but the rest is the same. He's not changing how he kills or what he does after, and that's all the evidence Jimmy needs to feel confident that the man who killed Lydia Rhodes is the same one who killed Cherish Spalding.

Jimmy jots some notes down in his notebook, returns the too-thin stack of documents to the box, closes the lid, and thanks the detective for his time.

"Well? Do we have another Ted Bundy on our hands?" The detective flashes him a grin.

Jimmy doesn't return the smile. "You'll want to call Salem PD," he says. "Ask to talk to Detective Michael Rausch. Tell him about this case. Tell him about Lydia's tongue being cut out. Maybe if the information comes from someone with a badge, he'll finally start paying attention."

As Jimmy brushes past the detective on his way out, he wonders what might have happened if someone in this department had given Lydia Rhodes more than ten minutes of their time. If the investigating detective hadn't looked down on her, brushed her off as another problem teenager in the wrong place, at the wrong time, making the wrong choices. If they'd tried even a little bit, maybe they could have caught the man who killed Lydia, and Cherish would still be alive. Not just Cherish, but all of the August girls.

Jimmy takes the I-5 freeway on-ramp north. The sun is a heavy orange ball dipping beneath the Coastal Range, spreading blue shadows across the Willamette Valley.

How many others, he wonders. *How many like Lydia are out there waiting to be found?*

The miles between Eugene and Salem are rural farmland interspersed with pockets of oak scrub and barns. There are so many hiding places, so many places too far from anywhere to hear a girl scream.

CHAPTER 7

Over the next six months, when Jimmy's not working on articles for the *Statesmen Journal*, he chases the stories of the August girls. He makes phone calls and crisscrosses the state, hunting for cold case murders that resemble Cherish and Lydia and the three others he knows about. During his time off, he sorts through evidence boxes with sour-smelling detectives sitting close by. He looks for girls of a certain age, strangled girls, girls with no names, forgotten girls with missing tongues or flowers in their hair.

When he finds one that fits his criteria, he writes her name down in a notebook, if she has one—so far, he's written Jane Doe more times than any other name. He also notes where she was found, the cause of death, and any known family members, or witnesses who spoke to the police, any suspects brought in for questioning. He writes down everything, even if it doesn't seem important.

His shoulders grow heavy and more slumped with each new girl he finds. Some small part of him hoped that when he started this search, he wouldn't find anything. He hoped he'd be laughed out of precincts, that the detectives he spoke to would send him off empty-handed, but every single time he's asked, the detective has nodded and said, "Yes, we have a case like that."

Jimmy takes pictures of whatever photograph is on file for the dead girl. Most often, it's an autopsy photo. Once, it was a mugshot because the dead girl had been picked up for solicitation a few months before she was killed. He brings each girl home and adds her to the wall in his apartment across from the fireplace.

A state road map takes up most of the space. He sticks thumbtacks into the places where the girls' bodies were found, looking for a pattern, finding none. One in Medford. One in Brownsville. Then Lydia Rhodes, who was killed in Eugene. Between 1970 and 1972, Jimmy finds no girls to match his criteria. Then in 1973, a girl was found dead in Bend, floating on her back in the Deschutes River, her hair tangled in the roots of a dead log, her hands clasped around a bouquet of Black-Eyed Susans. After that, he finds a Jane Doe in Gresham, a suburb of Portland, then number six in Corvallis, before the three Jane Does in Salem, and finally, the most recent August girl, Cherish Spalding.

Ten thumbtacks, two of them are blue, the rest are red. Two have names. The rest are nameless or known only by an alias, with no family to claim them. Whoever this monster is, he's smart enough to know that killing too often in the same place draws unwanted attention. So he moves from place to place, choosing women no one cares about, doing his best not to get caught.

"I'm worried about you," Jimmy's mother says every Sunday when he goes over to her house for dinner. "You're nothing but skin and bones. You look exhausted. Are you sure you're sleeping enough?"

He tries to sleep but ends up staring at the dark ceiling, listening to the scanner on his nightstand pop and crackle. A sound that usually lulls him to sleep, but recently, the hiss has become the voices of the ten dead women, their last gasping breaths rising in a crescendo. The shadows start to move and swirl around him, and then Cherish appears with her empty eyes and her gaping wounds, the maggots feasting. She opens her mouth. He sits up, waiting for her to speak, to tell him who did this to her, who did this to all of them. But what comes from the abyss of her mouth is that same steady hiss of the scanner, bringing him no answers.

Tadd humors Jimmy with the story, occasionally allowing an Ophelia Killer article onto the front-page, but there are only so many ways to write about an investigation that's going nowhere. People get bored. They stop seeing the boogeyman in every flickering shadow and lose interest. Cherish Spalding and the other women are buried deeper and deeper as more salacious news stories shove their way into headlines.

In November 1979, fifty-two American diplomats and citizens are taken hostage at the US Embassy in Iran. January ushers in a new decade and a recession. Six of the diplomats still being held hostage pose as Canadians and manage to escape. In February, the Winter Olympics begin in New York and, miracle of miracles, during the medal round of the men's hockey tournament, the United States beats the Soviet Union, four-time gold medal winners and heavily favored to win. It's the upset of the century, and all anyone wants to read about for weeks. In May, Mount Saint Helens erupts, killing 57 people and obliterating the entire north side of the mountain. Ash spreads thick over Southern Washington and into Oregon. The ash cloud then moves east, damaging crops and causing poor visibility across Washington, Idaho, Montana, and even into North Dakota. These are the stories making the front-page.

By June, no one is talking about Cherish Spalding anymore. No one cares about the Ophelia Killer, who may or may not even exist. No one cares except Jimmy, who grows more worried every day they inch closer to August. He calls the precinct every week to try and talk to Michael Rausch, but the detective never seems to be around. Annabeth apologizes and promises to give Rausch a message. Days fold into weeks fold into months, and still, Jimmy hears nothing back.

Then in July, eleven months after Cherish Spalding was found at Crocker Creek, Jimmy finally gets a call from Detective Rausch. "I heard you might have some information for me about this Spalding case?"

Jimmy's hopes rise again. They'll be cutting it pretty close, but they can still do it. They can catch this bastard before he kills again.

Jimmy suggests they meet at a coffee shop near the precinct, but Detective Rausch insists on coming to Jimmy's apartment. "This isn't the kind of conversation I want to have in public," he says.

"I can come to the precinct, then," Jimmy says. "Or we can use a conference room at the *Statesman*."

Rausch laughs into the phone. "You got something over there you don't want me to see?"

Two hours later, Detective Michael Rausch is standing in Jimmy's living room, staring at the wall of maps, thumbtacks, and dead women. He whistles softly through his teeth. "I heard rumors you were tracking this guy, but this looks more like an obsession."

"I'm just trying to find patterns, connections, see if something was overlooked in these earlier kills that might lead us to him." Jimmy goes to the wall and points at the four thumbtacks clustered around Salem. "These appear to be his most recent kills." He moves his finger to a red thumbtack near Medford. "This one, in 1967? I think this might have been his first. He seems to have taken a break between 1970 and 1972, so maybe he was in prison or something? If he's been in the system, that could help us. There weren't fingerprints at any of the other scenes, but maybe there were some found on Cherish?"

Jimmy turns toward Rausch, hoping for the man's input, but Rausch isn't paying attention. He's wandering through the apartment, lifting framed photographs off tables, inspecting the pictures inside, flipping through magazines and books.

"Detective?"

Rausch looks up with a thin-lipped grin. "You know, you really should offer a man something to drink before you start talking dirty."

Jimmy shoves down the urge to kick Rausch out of the apartment. You catch more bees with honey, his mother's always telling him. He returns Rausch's tight smile and says, "I've got water."

"I'm a whiskey man myself." His smug grin twists tighter. "Got any of that?"

Jimmy walks the three steps that separate the living room from the kitchen. He finds the bottle of whiskey he keeps in a cupboard on top of the fridge. It was a gift from Tadd after Jimmy landed his first front-page story six years ago. The bottle's still three-quarters full. He pours the detective a healthy dose.

"Want ice?" Jimmy calls to Rausch.

"Do I want you to water down my whiskey?" Rausch calls back, his voice slightly muffled. "What kind of man do you take me for, Slim Jim?"

When Jimmy steps back into the living room, he finds Rausch digging through the hall closet near the front door. Jimmy clears his throat. Rausch steps back, still smiling like he wasn't caught snooping through another man's things.

"Looking for something in particular?" Jimmy asks.

The closet door is still open. Rausch jerks his thumb at the coats. "Are these all the jackets you have? Got anymore hanging in your bedroom?"

"What? Why?"

"Ever worn a pea coat? You know the bulky wool ones with

wide collars, big buttons." Rausch closes the closet door, takes two long strides to where Jimmy is standing, plucks the whiskey from his hand, and keeps walking into the kitchen. "What about the military? You ever been in the Navy? Coast Guard? You're about the right age to have been called up in the draft."

"Not that it's any of your business, but I got an academic deferment," Jimmy says, following Rausch.

The detective flips open cupboards and pulls open drawers, looking for something, though Jimmy doesn't know what. "Ever work on a fishing boat?"

"Why are you asking me these questions?" Jimmy steps in front of Rausch to keep him from opening any more cupboard doors. "And why the hell are you searching my apartment without a warrant?"

This time when Rausch smiles, he flashes teeth. "Don't get your panties in a bunch, Slim Jim. I'm a curious guy, that's all. Like you. You're a curious guy, too, aren't you?"

He tips the whiskey to his lips and makes a satisfied hissing sound as the alcohol rolls down his throat. His second sip is more like a gulp, and he might as well be drinking water. His eyes dart toward the sliding glass door that leads out to a small balcony off the kitchen.

"You able to keep that thing alive?" Rausch points at a potted cactus sitting in the sun.

"So far, so good," Jimmy answers. "Now, are you going to tell me what's going on with this coat business?"

Rausch ignores him and steps close to the glass. The balcony overlooks a small and tidy lawn behind the apartment complex. Within walking distance, there's a shallow pond thick with reeds. Some days, the pond's entire surface is covered in ducks, but today there are only three. A green-headed mallard and his two brown-speckled ladies.

"Got any fish in there?" Rausch asks.

"Just frogs."

"Too bad. You a fishing kind of man, Slim Jim?" His eyes stay focused on the pond and the ducks paddling in circles.

"Not much. Went a few times with my grandpa as a kid, but I never took to it."

"Too bad."

"I always felt sorry for the fish," Jimmy adds. "I always wanted to let them go."

Rausch turns away from the glass and studies Jimmy. There's a moment where neither man speaks, then Rausch breaks his gaze and marches back into the living room to study the wall instead.

"So tell me, Slim Jim." He takes a long drink of whiskey, nearly draining the glass. "Who am I looking for here?"

Jimmy stands next to him in front of the wall. "Well, he seems organized. Careful. Until Cherish, the victims he chose were women who wouldn't be missed. Vulnerable women who wouldn't put up much of a fight. He leaves his crime scenes clean, dumps the bodies near water, in places where people aren't likely to stumble upon them for a few days, weeks, months sometimes, after any good physical evidence has long been degraded. He's probably educated or has some idea of how police investigate crimes, so he knows how to avoid detection. He's changing his pattern, though." Jimmy gestures to the four thumbtacks centered around Salem. "He's not moving around as much anymore. And Cherish doesn't fit his typical victim profile. She wasn't just someone he picked up off the side of the road, like the others, a woman in the wrong place at the wrong time. From what her roommates told me, he was hunting her. He watched her from the street, maybe even followed her to campus. We should ask around, find out if anyone noticed a strange man paying Cherish particular attention in the months before her death."

"What else do you think *we* should do?" Rausch asks.

Jimmy speaks quickly, pushing aside his dislike of the detective for the sake of the case. "It's pretty clear that there are at least nine other women we can connect to Cherish Spalding's case. Ten women killed by the same person. And there may be more I haven't found yet. You have to expand your search, ask for more resources, get a special unit going. You need to start working with the other departments, too. Expand outside of the Salem PD. That's how they caught Ted Bundy."

"You think this guy is another Ted Bundy?" Rausch's laugh is sharp and caustic. He swirls the last of the whiskey in the bottom of the glass before gulping it back. "That would be pretty good for you, now, wouldn't it?"

"What do you mean? How could it possibly be good for me?"

"Those articles you wrote last summer, what did you call him? The Ophelia Killer? How many papers did you sell because of that? Now, think of the headline if you were to help catch him." Rausch swings his hand through the air in an arc. "Small town reporter captures the next Ted Bundy. You'd be famous, Slim Jim. Isn't that what this is all about?" He gestures at the wall. "Isn't that why you're doing all this? For the front-page story? The book deal? The morning show appearances?"

Of course, Jimmy's thought about it. He's only human. Reeling in that kind of story could open a lot of doors for him, but it's about more than that, too. The women who were killed deserve justice. The people who love those women deserve answers. The communities where those women lived deserve to be able to fall asleep at night without worrying if their daughters are next.

"I just want him stopped before he kills someone else," Jimmy says.

"He's not as smart as Ted Bundy, you know." Rausch sets the empty glass down on the coffee table.

"Why do you say that?"

Rausch moves close to the wall. He traces a finger over one of the photographs of Cherish Spalding. It's the one Jimmy took of her laid out at Crocker Creek before the detective showed up.

"He left something behind," Rausch says, stepping away from the wall again.

"What is it?" Jimmy can't keep the excitement from leaping to his voice, even as he tries to push it down.

This is big. This changes everything. Physical evidence proves the person killing these women isn't some phantom, a mythical swamp creature preying on innocent girls who stray too far from the highway. Physical evidence proves he's human. Humans make mistakes. Mistakes are how they will catch him.

Rausch cocks his head. "You know I can't tell you that."

"I'm on your side here, Rausch. I know these cases inside and out. I know them better than anyone."

"Yes, you certainly do."

"If what you found is connected to these other cases, that could be enough to convince your chief of police to put a bigger team together. Call in the FBI even."

"I don't need the FBI's help."

"Are you sure about that?" Jimmy asks. "Last time I checked, you didn't even have any suspects."

"Police don't tell the press everything, Slim Jim. We don't tell our receptionists everything either." The words crackle with anger. "I have a suspect, actually. And I'm looking at him right now."

Laughter bubbles up in Jimmy's chest, a choked, sputtering sound. "Are you kidding me? You think I did this?"

"Can you blame me?" He gestures to the wall. "I walk in here and find this...what is this? A shrine? A wall of memories? You can see how a person might get the wrong idea about your interest in this case, can't you?"

"I've kept you in the loop about everything I've found. I tried to bring you in on this months ago, but you ignored my calls."

"I'm a busy man, Slim Jim." Rausch spreads his hands in the air.

"What could possibly be more important than finding Cherish's killer?" Jimmy asks through clenched teeth.

"Tell me something," Rausch says, ignoring Jimmy's question. "You were first on the scene with the Spalding girl, weren't you? Got there before my guys did, even. That seems pretty convenient, doesn't it? The way you seem to know what's going on before anyone else does? I asked around about you, Slim Jim, don't think I didn't. You know what everyone told me? That Cherish Spalding isn't the only time you've been one of the first people to show up to a scene. That you seem to have a knack for knowing where dead girls are going to turn up."

"I'm just paying attention," Jimmy says. "Which is more than you seem to be doing."

Rausch's lips pull back in a smile caught somewhere between amusement and distaste. "You know, I heard this story once. About a firefighter who started his own fires. He'd set these fires all over town. Then he'd swoop in with his lights and sirens and save the day. He liked being the hero. The rush of it. He was addicted to the adrenaline, the power of being the one who kept people from being burned alive in the houses he set on fire."

"This is ridiculous." Jimmy flings his hands in the air. "I didn't kill Cherish or anyone else, and that's the last time I'm going to say it. If you have proof that says the opposite, arrest me. Otherwise, there's the door. Kindly show yourself out."

Rausch crosses the room.

When he reaches the door, Jimmy says, "If you don't throw every single resource you have behind this case over the next few weeks, another girl is going to die."

Rausch turns to look over his shoulder. Sweat glints on his broad forehead. "Is that a threat, Mr. Eagan?"

"No, Detective Rausch." Jimmy lays emphasis on the man's title. "It's the plain and simple truth."

Rausch shakes his head and leaves. The door slams shut behind him.

———

After Rausch's visit, Jimmy calls Annabeth every day to check on the progress of the investigation, and every day Annabeth says the same thing. "I don't know anything about anything anymore, Jimmy. They all clam up when I come into the room. They don't want me talking to you. I'm sorry. I wish I could help."

After a week of this, Annabeth answers his call on the verge of tears. "Jimmy, you've got to stop calling here, okay? I'm going to get fired."

So Jimmy stops calling. Rausch knows what's at stake; he just doesn't seem to care. Getting Annabeth in trouble isn't going to help anything.

August arrives with a clap of thunder. It rains for almost a week straight, with thunderheads rolling through every night, rattling the windows and setting the neighborhood dogs howling. The hair on Jimmy's arms refuses to lie flat. He tries to distract himself with work, with other stories, but finds himself going back over his notes on the August girls and waiting for the call to come over the police scanner.

After the storms pass, the entire valley is weighted down by sweltering heat that won't break. Even the nights are sticky and warm, the temperatures never dipping below sixty-five. During the day, it's over a hundred degrees in the shade.

On those hottest nights, when Jimmy can't sleep, he goes to the house where Cherish used to live with her two friends. Starting from the end of their driveway, he walks in circles around the block, expanding ever outward, hoping to stumble upon something or someone. A shadow lurking in the corners, a clue that will send him to the right place before it's too late. A part of him is out here, too, because he is scared for Cherish's roommates, and all the other girls living in different houses up and down this street. He doesn't want another one to turn up dead. Though he knows it will happen, that for as long as the man who killed Cherish Spalding is free, he will keep killing. But the nights when Jimmy is out here, his footsteps echoing in the dark, he wants to believe he can protect them.

He keeps the scanner close beside him, shuffling it between work and home, listening to every crackle and pop, but the only codes called are for domestic violence, burglaries, and suspicious persons.

As the end of August draws near, Jimmy begins to wonder if the Ophelia Killer left Salem, if maybe there won't be a dead girl this year after all.

In one week, it'll be September, and maybe the heat will finally turn autumn cool. But until then, the air conditioning in the press room is broken, and Jimmy's suffering through it and trying not to think about what it would mean if the Ophelia Killer isn't close by anymore.

Jimmy's shirt is drenched in sweat. The small fan clipped to the corner of his desk does nothing but blow hot air across his already flaming skin. He rises from his chair, thinking he'll go to the convenience store down the street and buy the rest of the crew popsicles. Before he even takes a step, the phone on his desk rings.

It's Annabeth. She's sniffling, breathless. "They're not putting it out on the radio. Mike doesn't want a circus showing up, but Jimmy, you have to go, you have to—" Her voice cracks around a sob. "They found another one, Jimmy. Out near Valentine Creek. They found another girl like Cherish."

Chapter 8

Jimmy parks behind a line of green and white sheriff's cars. After a quick scan of the road and the officers waiting in the nearby field, he can see no one from Salem PD or Rausch's team has arrived yet.

According to Annabeth, or at least from what Jimmy could piece together through her sporadic sobbing, the body was found outside the city limits, and the county sheriff responded first. When the deputies realized what they were dealing with, they made a discreet call to the Salem PD and asked for Detective Michael Rausch. Everyone locally knows he's the one in charge of dead girls now. No one else wants to touch this.

Jimmy didn't speed to get here. He didn't take any shortcuts because there are no shortcuts. The only way to get to Valentine Creek is to head east on Highway 22 toward Silver Creek Falls, take the Fern Ridge Road exit, and drive through rolling empty farmland for a few miles. He heard the news from Annabeth after Rausch got the sheriff's call, and yet somehow, he still beat the detective here.

After last month's disaster of a conversation at his apartment, Jimmy knows how showing up first is going to look. Showing up at all is probably a bad idea, but neither can he stay away. He stares over the field where the sheriff's deputies are waiting in a loose circle near a clump of fir and ash trees.

It's nearly identical to the place where they found Cherish Spalding. An expanse of tilled earth edged with trees. Dust devils spin across the barren field. Inside the green shadows of the woods, Jimmy knows there'll be a trickle of water, a creek if it's wide enough. That's where the girl will be, too, tucked inside those thirsty limbs, sheltered from the baking sun and prying eyes.

Knuckles rap on the driver's side window. Jimmy startles and whips his head around. A young woman in a tan uniform, with a forest green windbreaker pulled over her shoulders, peers into his car. A sheriff's star is embroidered onto the jacket's left breast pocket, but there's no name badge visible.

Jimmy swings his eyes up to her face, suddenly embarrassed that he was looking at her chest, but she doesn't seem to notice. Her brown hair is pulled back into a low, tight bun, revealing sharply angled cheekbones and a prominent forehead. She squints at him through the glass. Her hand hovers close to the service weapon strapped to her hips.

"You lost?" she shouts through the window.

Jimmy fumbles in his seat for his press badge and holds it up with what he hopes is a disarming smile.

The woman's glare hardens. She straightens and takes a step back, swinging her head around like she's looking for someone else to pass him off to. Jimmy takes the opportunity to crack open the car door and get out.

"I'm Jimmy," he says, but she ignores him.

In the six years working the crime beat for the *Statesmen Journal*, she's the first woman he's seen in uniform. He knows women who work with the force, civilians like Annabeth, but he's never met a woman wearing a badge.

"You're new, right? I've shown up to a lot of these, and I've never seen you before." He laughs lightly, talking to her the way he talks to everyone else, easy, friendly.

But she's not everyone else. She swings her gaze to him. Her eyes are a dark blue, swirling with shreds of gray fog.

"This is an active crime scene." Her voice is tense enough to shatter. "Stay out of the way."

She spins away from him and marches back to her post in front of the perimeter tape strung along a barbed-wire fence delineating the field from the gravel berm. She's been assigned crowd control. There's no crowd now, but there will be. News like this spreads faster than a rash. Soon enough, the road will be crowded with TV news vans and other reporters like Jimmy.

The female deputy stands with her back to the trees and the half-dozen men in matching tan shirts waiting in the field for someone to tell them what to do. She stares into the distance, her face as stony and unmoved as the pebbles beneath her heavy boots. She keeps her arms folded over her chest, her back straight and bristling. There's no softness in her except the curve of her hips.

An unmarked car parks on the road behind Jimmy's car. He tears his eyes away from the woman and walks to meet Detective Rausch, who unfolds himself from the driver's seat and cracks his neck. "What the hell are you doing here?"

He doesn't sound angry, just bored. He moves his gaze away from Jimmy to the female deputy standing by the perimeter tape. His tongue darts across his lips. "Who's that?"

He doesn't wait for Jimmy's answer.

With Jimmy close on his heels, Rausch strides over to the deputy and leans in too close. "It's a crime to look that good in a deputy's uniform, you know. Shame. I might have to arrest you."

She steps back. Rausch steps forward, devouring the gap. "You need my name, right? How about I give you my phone number, too. But don't call too late on weeknights. My wife wouldn't like it very much."

The deputy grits her teeth and reaches to lift the yellow tape. "Go ahead, Detective Rausch." She says his name in a way that sounds like 'roach,' and the hard flint of her eyes tells Jimmy she's deliberately mispronouncing it. "They're all waiting for you down there."

She gestures to where the other deputies are standing near the trees.

Rausch glares at her for half a second, then huffs a loud breath and ducks under the perimeter. Jimmy starts to follow him, but Rausch presses a hand to his chest, keeping him back. He laughs. "Yeah, I don't think so, Slim Jim. The last thing I need is you underfoot, mucking up my crime scene. You can wait here with the missus. Depending on what I find down there, I might want to talk to you anyway, so don't stray too far."

Detective Rausch walks down the sloped berm toward the trees with long strides and a swagger in his step.

"What a creep." The deputy mutters it under her breath.

Jimmy flattens the smile tugging on his lips and pretends he didn't hear her. "Did you say something?"

She flashes him a glance and shifts slightly away from him.

Jimmy lets a few seconds of silence pass before he says, "So. A woman deputy. You don't see that every day."

She says nothing, but her nostrils flare.

"What made you join up? Let me guess. Your father was a cop?"

Her gaze slides over to him. There's nothing nice swimming in her eyes.

"Is this an interview?" Her voice is clipped, still pissed off about Rausch. Understandably.

"Not if you don't want it to be." He shoves his hands in his pockets and digs a toe into the ground. "I'm just curious about how someone like you ends up in a den full of wolves. It can't be easy dealing with assholes like Rausch all day long."

She grimaces and turns her gaze back to the field across the road. "Thank God they're not all like Rausch."

Another silent minute passes. Without turning her eyes from the trees, the deputy says, "I know who you are. I've read your articles."

"Oh good," Jimmy says. "Then you're well aware that I'm full of crap."

The laugh surprises him. It's a horse snort. Loud and immodest. He feels his heart flutter in a way he hasn't ever felt it flutter before, and for the briefest of moments, he worries he's having a heart attack. Then the feeling passes. He slides a bashful grin in her direction. "How long have you been a deputy for?"

"About a year." There's a hint of pride in her voice. "I was a correction's officer before this. But I was getting tired of being stuck inside all day."

Her whole body tenses, her focus shifting again to the opposite field, to a small clump of trees twisted with shadows and blackberry vines. "Did you see that?"

Jimmy squints but sees nothing unusual.

"I think there's someone over there." Her hand reaches for her gun, and then she's bounding away from him, taking off in a streak of tan polyester. The gravel crunches under her boots as she darts across the road and disappears into the trees.

Jimmy can hear her shouting at someone to stop. "Police! Get down on the ground!"

He glances in the direction of Detective Rausch, but the man is tucked out of sight in the trees near the creek, and none of the other deputies are close enough for Jimmy to wave over for assistance. Another shout echoes in the distance, and it sounds like someone might be hurt. Jimmy darts across the road, shoving through the bushes where the deputy disappeared only a few moments before.

He ducks beneath a low-hanging branch and pushes through

thorny vines, chasing the sounds of crashing brush ahead of him. Noises echo all around, loud in every direction. He quickly becomes turned around in the tangled vegetation. He pushes forward anyway, trying to get closer to the panting sound of someone running, the swift thump of footsteps against the hard earth. He breaks into a small clearing and stops for a second to catch his breath and get his bearings again.

The clearing is small enough he could spread his arms wide and touch every leaf. He spins in a circle, listening for sounds, trying to decide which direction to go in. There hasn't been any more shouting since he entered the thicket. He doesn't know if the deputy's hurt or if she's given up the chase and gone back to the road.

Behind him, branches crack. He turns toward the sound, bracing himself for whatever beast is barreling through the trees straight for him.

The crash knocks the wind out of him. He ends up on his back on the ground with a long-haired, wild man on top of him, pummeling fists, grunting and snorting like a mad raccoon. Spittle drips onto Jimmy's face. Jimmy bucks and squirms and tries to get his hands free to protect himself, but the man pins his arms with his knees. He's got at least thirty pounds on Jimmy, too, and a fear in eyes that borders on rage. Whatever this man is running from, he's desperate not to be caught, and Jimmy understands quite clearly that he will not hesitate to kill.

Jimmy goes limp, hoping that by playing dead, the man will get bored and decide to leave on his own, but it doesn't work. The man's fists keep raining down on Jimmy's face, blow after blow until his head is ringing and he sees stars. The whole world lights up with the bright explosions coming from inside his skull.

Suddenly, the man is wrenched back. From where Jimmy lays sprawled in the dirt, it looks as if the man is flying away from him, pulled back by some supernatural force. Jimmy stays on the ground, feeling his fingers over his body, checking to see that he's still in one piece.

Nearby, there's a crashing sound and a loud grunt, then the hissing of breath through teeth and a woman saying, "Hold still, you piece of shit." A clatter and clank of metal. Then more rustling of leaves and brambles. "Goddamn it. Sit there and don't fucking move." A breath puffed out in victory, then she's standing over Jimmy with her hands on her hips. A dark silhouette against the gray sky, a goddamn superhero.

She reaches one hand toward him. "Are you all right?"

Jimmy lets her help him to his feet. He groans. The world seems to be spinning too fast. There's a copper taste in his mouth, the bitter salt of his own blood.

"Easy does it," she says and wraps her arms around his waist to keep him steady. "You took quite the hit."

"I got the shit kicked out of me."

That laugh again, but softer now, edged in concern. "Can you stand on your own?"

He tests his weight, finds he's more stable than he thought he was. There's a sharp pain in his ribcage. The rest of him feels like he was hit by a truck. But he can breathe, he can stand, he can take a small step. The stars in his skull have fizzled to nothing. The ringing in his ears is still there, but not as loud as before. He flicks his gaze to where the man now sits against the trunk of a tree, breathing heavily, his eyes still wild, but he sits. He stays. His hands are cuffed behind his back. He bares his teeth at Jimmy and lets out a growl.

"Who is he?" Jimmy asks.

The deputy goes over to the man and kicks the side of his leg. The man yelps.

"Who are you?" she asks. "What are you doing out here?"

The man glares at her but says nothing.

She bends close to his face. "There's a dead girl barely a hundred yards from where I found you."

The man's eyes widen as he tries to pull away from her. He wrestles against his cuffs, sputtering, "I didn't—I didn't—"

"Now. Are you going to tell me who the hell you are and what you're doing lurking around these woods, or am I just going to assume you're the one who killed that girl?" The deputy throws her arm in the direction of the road.

The man slumps his head against his chest. He whispers something.

"Where did you leave them?" the deputy asks, making no attempt to hide the disgust in her voice.

The man tips his chin to a section of the thicket where, if Jimmy squints, he can see a faint footpath. "Follow that to the creek."

The deputy grabs the man by the elbow and jerks him to his feet. She shoves him ahead of her as she ducks out of the clearing and into the trees. Jimmy spits blood into the dirt and limps after them. As they walk through the trees, the deputy talks to Jimmy over her shoulder.

"This guy's a real winner. Says his dog had puppies last week, and he couldn't think of anything better to do with them than bring them out here and dump them. What do you think? Sounds like a load of shit, if you ask me. Ten bucks says we won't find any puppies."

But as soon as they get close to the creek, they hear faint whimpering.

The deputy walks faster to get to the black garbage sack sitting half in the creek and half on the bank. She shoves the man to one side. He stumbles over his own feet and almost falls, catching himself against the trunk of a tree at the last second.

Jimmy rushes to the deputy's side, crouching to help her drag the garbage sack onto dry ground. She takes a pocket knife from her utility belt and cuts the bag open. Six puppies spill and tumble into the dirt. Their eyes are barely open. Their faces wrinkly, their ears floppy. They're wobbly on their feet, able to stand only for a few seconds before toppling over again. They bump against one another, whimpering and whining. Two of them find Jimmy's hand and begin nuzzling it. They're velvety soft, dark brown with white spots and some brown on their paws, and goddamn it, but they're the cutest creatures he's ever seen in his whole life.

The deputy curses under her breath and turns to the man in handcuffs. "Do you know anything about the girl?"

"I told you, I don't know nothing about no girl. I didn't hear nothing. I didn't see nothing. I didn't touch her."

The deputy returns her attention to the puppies. She seems to be trying to decide what to do. Jimmy takes off his button-down shirt. He's got a white and threadbare T-shirt on underneath, which isn't the most attractive piece of clothing but better than nothing. He lays the nicer shirt on the ground. One by one, checking each puppy for injury, he settles them into the shirt, bundling them all together in a warm squirming pouch that he holds against his chest. "I'll take care of them."

Sweat glistens on the deputy's brow. Her hair is starting to come loose. She sweeps a hank of it behind her ear. "Just get them back to the road, and I can call county animal services to handle them."

But Jimmy knows what happens to dogs who get sent to the county shelter. The puppies are so light in his arms, barely the weight of a bag of flour. "I said I'll take care of them."

He turns away from her and walks back through the trees, careful with the makeshift pouch, making sure none of the pups accidentally slip out. Behind him, he hears the deputy talking to the man again, then the heavy fall of their footsteps as they follow him.

When they get to the road, Jimmy settles the puppies in his

car's back seat. The deputy shoves the handcuffed man into the back of a patrol car. She issues a couple of sharp commands into her radio, then turns toward Jimmy.

"Thanks for your help back there." Her eyes have darkened with the rush of the chase. There's something feral in them that draws Jimmy a step closer.

"I should be the one thanking you," he says.

"He would have gotten away if you hadn't thrown yourself into his fists." Her hand lifts, not touching him, just brushing the air inches above his cheek. "You're gonna want to get some ice on that before it swells up so bad you can't see."

He crouches to look at his face in the reflection of his car window. The skin around his right eye is split. Blood seeps down his cheek. Already it's starting to swell, the skin around his socket turning purple. His hand lifts automatically. He flinches from even that gentle pressure. He doesn't think it's broken, though.

The deputy peers through the window at the puppies now tumbling out of the shirt and sniffing Jimmy's car. "You sure about this? I can still call animal control."

"Don't bother," Jimmy says. One of the puppies, the only one with four matching, white paws, stares at him through the glass. "I know a guy who loves dogs. He's constantly bringing in strays. He also happens to be a veterinarian. He'll be happy to look them over and make sure they're okay before he finds good homes for them."

The deputy studies Jimmy for a moment, then nods, satisfied, and flicks her gaze toward the man sitting in the back of the patrol car.

"You think he's telling the truth? About not being involved with all of this?" She waves her hand toward the field where the deputies have spread out, searching for evidence.

"It seems like a pretty big coincidence, him showing up here," Jimmy says.

"That's what I thought, too."

Before they can discuss it further, two vans pull up on the side of the road. One is the silver coroner's van. The other is from KOIN news. The deputy hitches her shoulders back, the edges of her sharpening again as she jerks her chin toward the vans. "Better get back to work before the Roach writes me up for insubordination."

"Maybe I'll see you around." Jimmy lets the words hang between them like a question.

"No offense," she says with a flicker of a smile. "But I really hope not."

She leaves him with the puppies and walks toward the vans. Jimmy realizes too late that he never asked for her name.

CHAPTER 9

The newest August girl found near Valentine Creek turns out to be another Willamette University student. Her name is Natasha Tinneford. Like Cherish, she was a freshman. Like Cherish, she lived away from her family. This time, though, her parents are in a completely different state, some small town in Wisconsin. They apparently hadn't seen or spoken to their daughter in several months before they got the call, which wasn't unusual, according to them. Natasha was always an independent child. She was captain of the rowing team, strong and compact, her long brown hair streaked with blond. According to her friends, her sense of humor was wry and cutting. She hadn't yet declared a major, but the people Jimmy talks to say she was leaning toward a law degree. They also say this should never have happened to her.

Jimmy keeps hearing this phrase or something similar. Natasha was always cautious. She never drank too much at parties, never walked home alone at night, never took strange boys back to her dorm room. No, this should never have happened to a girl who carried a pocket knife in her jeans and a whistle bracelet around her wrist.

In the days following Natasha Tinneford's death, Jimmy tries to get information about the case from the sheriff's office. They send him to the Salem Police central precinct to talk to Rausch, but Rausch won't give him the time of day, and so Jimmy goes back across town to the sheriff's office, only to be told again that they don't have any information about the case.

He lingers in the lobby, hoping he'll run into the deputy with the daring blue eyes, but no matter what time he shows up, she's never there. By October, he's beginning to think he imagined her and the chase in the woods, the wild man, the sack of puppies. Except he's got a small scar over his right eyebrow that every day fades a little more and a twelve-week-old beagle puppy eating him out of house and home.

She's the smallest of the litter, the runt with four white paws. Jimmy's friend didn't give her very good odds to live through her first night, but then she did. And she lived through the next night, too, and the night after that, growing bigger and stronger every day. Jimmy visited the puppies often and, when they were old enough, his friend asked if he wanted to take one home. He chose the runt, the one who wasn't supposed to survive. He names her Trixie after the sleuth in the books his mother used to read him as a boy.

Between work and caring for Trixie, Jimmy loses track of time until one day he blinks, and suddenly it's New Year's Eve. It's been five months since Natasha Tinneford's body was found, and no arrests have been made. But there is some good news.

A special unit is finally organized to investigate Cherish, Natasha, and the three other Salem women's deaths together as one case, hunting one killer. The team, led by Detective Michael Rausch, sets up their offices in an old bank building next to the central precinct.

Every day for the entire month of January, Jimmy stands on the sidewalk outside with Trixie and tries to get someone to talk to him about the case. More than two dozen people come in and out of the building each day. Most of them Jimmy recognizes as officers from the Salem PD and sheriff's deputies from Marion County. There are other people, too, people Jimmy has never seen before. Men with well-fitted, expensive-looking suits who might be from the Bureau. It doesn't matter whether he knows them or not; every single person brushes past him like he's a stray dog begging for scraps. They pretend he's not even there.

Detective Rausch holds dull press conferences every Friday, and every Friday, he says the same few sentences. "We are continuing to investigate the homicides of Cherish Spalding and Natasha Tinneford. We are considering several other homicides in the area to be related. At this time, we do not believe the public is in any immediate danger. Still, we strongly suggest young women between the ages of sixteen and thirty travel in pairs or groups, especially at night. We continue to ask for the public's help with this ongoing investigation." Then he reads off the tip line phone number for people to call if they have any information.

Jimmy tries to corner Rausch after each press conference, but the detective brushes him off, refusing to give him even the briefest quote. The articles Jimmy writes for the *Statesman Journal* become repetitive, and it's hard to convince Tadd to keep the girls on the front-page. It's an election year, and Ronald Regan is sworn in as the fortieth President of the United States. The Iranian government agrees to release the American hostages after fourteen months. There are other tragedies, too, other shootings, death, and violence that have nothing to do with the Ophelia Killer. Jimmy watches helplessly as, once again, the August girls fade from the public's mind.

Feeling sorry for himself, powerless, staring at the calendar, watching the days tick closer to another August, another dead girl, Jimmy takes Trixie with him into the bar across the street from the old bank building where Rausch's special unit seems to be doing nothing but spinning their wheels.

Trixie is almost six months old now, but she's still all floppy ears and folded skin, with dewy brown eyes that are hard to say no to. Jimmy sneaks her into the bar under his coat and picks a booth hidden in the corner where he hopes no one will notice her and where he doesn't have to watch the college frat boys drink and hit on girls.

The jukebox thumps the floorboards, the song scratchy but familiar. Jimmy shucks peanuts and sips cheap beer. Trixie curls up on the bench beside him, cozying up against his leg. The song changes. The front door swings open, swings shut, and a blast of cold night air blows in behind the woman who enters.

She's dressed in gray slacks that flare at the ankle and a navy shirt with puffy sleeves and a floppy piece of fabric around the neck that looks like it's trying to be a tie. Jimmy almost doesn't recognize her without the deputy's uniform. She stands a minute in the entryway, scanning the bar like she's meeting someone here. Her eyes catch Jimmy's and flare wide with surprise. He feels like a lurker, in this corner booth, hunched over his beer, staring back at her like she's the best damn thing he's seen all day. He flashes a smile and lifts his hand in greeting. She tugs on the shirt, like it's uncomfortable, then crosses to his booth.

She opens her mouth to say something, then stops when she sees Trixie's little head pop up above the edge of the table. Whatever she was going to say is forgotten. "Is that one from Valentine Creek?" she asks instead and slides into the empty booth across from them without waiting for an invitation.

Jimmy doesn't mind. His heart is thumping so hard, he's worried it might be loud enough for her to hear. He never thought he'd see her again, and now here she is, and the man who has never once been at a loss for words in his whole life can't think of a single thing to say to her.

She reaches to scratch Trixie's chin. "I can't believe you kept one. You did just keep one, right? You don't have a whole basket of puppies under the table?"

She laughs softly, and the sound breaks Jimmy's trance. He laughs along with her. "No basket of puppies. I can barely keep up with this little imp."

Trixie decides now is a good time to chew on Jimmy's shirt sleeve.

Jimmy plucks his shirt from her needle-sharp teeth and says, "If I had known she'd be this much trouble, I would have left her with my friend."

"I don't believe you."

"You're right. I mean, look at her." He scoops Trixie off the bench and holds her in the air. Her white paws kick as she wiggles and squirms, trying to get free.

The deputy reaches out her hand. Trixie licks her fingers. The deputy's smile is soft enough to break Jimmy's heart. Her eyes are blue enough to drown in. He curses himself silently for getting so caught up in a woman whose name he doesn't even know.

Jimmy settles Trixie into his lap. The puppy circles once before curling into a ball, tucking her nose under her tail, and falling asleep. He thinks they have about two or three more months before she'll be too big to fit.

"Well, I'm glad to see it all worked out," the deputy says, settling in herself, relaxing against the seat as if she's going to stay awhile.

"You know," Jimmy says. "I don't think I properly thanked you for saving my life. Let me buy you a beer. Or a glass of wine, if you prefer?"

He glances at the bar, hoping to catch the bartender's attention, but the man is busy with those frat boys who are trying to convince him to sell them the entire bottle of tequila.

"Thanks, but—" She points to the badge clipped on her belt. "I don't drink when I'm on-duty."

Jimmy picks up the menu that's been lying in front of him since he got here. "Then how about dinner? A salad or something?"

She rolls her eyes and, when a server finally shows up at their booth, says, "Can I get some chili cheese fries? And a Coke? Put it on his tab." She jerks her thumb at Jimmy, who smiles at the server and nods that it's okay.

The server flicks a glance at Trixie sleeping in Jimmy's lap but says nothing.

When the server leaves, the deputy shakes her head and says, "I probably should eat something with a little more nutrition, but this job, man. I deserve something greasy and delicious after all the shit I've had to put up with today."

"You're working across the street?" Jimmy asks on a hunch.

She nods. "They have me answering phones like a glorified secretary," she says with a laugh and gestures at her outfit. "But at least I don't have to wear my uniform, which, by the way, is made of wool and not the nice kind of wool, but the kind your grandmother knits your Christmas sweaters out of because she likes to torture you."

Jimmy laughs, and her cheeks flush. She ducks her head, but he can see she's smiling, that she's pleased with herself for being the kind of funny that gets a reaction.

"You never told me your name." Jimmy lifts his elbows to rest on the table, careful not to jostle Trixie too much.

The deputy looks him up and down as if trying to decide whether or not to tell him. Finally, she says, "It's Brett," and before he can say anything, she adds, "And yes, I know it's a boy's name."

"I wasn't going to say that."

"It's all right if you were. Everyone else does."

He shakes his head. "You shouldn't put words in other people's mouths." But he says it playfully, with a smile, so she knows he doesn't mean it.

She flicks her hand at his face. "Your eye is looking better."

The swelling lasted a few days, the bruising went away after a week. Six months later, and the scar is almost completely gone.

"What happened to him?" Jimmy asks. "The guy you arrested out there. Did you ever find out if he knew more than he was saying? I asked around, but no one at the office could tell me."

"Oh, I know all about you hanging around the offices." She tosses the words to him lightly, teasing.

Now it's Jimmy's turn to blush. His cheeks flame. The corner of Brett's mouth lifts in a half-smile. Despite himself, Jimmy is desperate to say something to make the other corner turn up, too. He wants to see her whole smile, feel the heat of it beaming directly at him.

"The bastard lawyered up," Brett adds. "But I'm pretty sure he's not the guy we're looking for. I'm pretty sure he's just a good-for-nothing dog dumper. Apparently, he was serving time for criminal trespass last August when Cherish Spalding was killed. So, if these two cases are truly connected, then he's not our guy."

The server returns to their booth at that moment with a sweating Coke and a greasy plate of chili fries, the cheese on top slick and hot. Brett unrolls a fork from a napkin and digs in like it's the first thing she's eaten all day. "So good," she says and gestures with her fork. "Want some?"

Jimmy pinches a fry with his fingertips and pops it in his mouth. Trixie lifts her head, but when she realizes she's not getting anything, she plops it down again, exhaling an indignant sigh.

"You know, I'm kind of surprised that you signed up to work on Rausch's team," Jimmy says.

Brett shrugs. "It's an interesting case."

"But is it interesting enough to put up with that asshole?"

Her eyes flick to his. "You know it is."

Quickly, she looks back down at the fries, eating a few bites before saying, "They shoved me into a corner by the bathrooms anyway, so it's not like I ever really see him. And I only have to talk to him if I go looking for a conversation."

"How's it going? With the investigation, I mean? Rausch is keeping pretty tight-lipped about the whole thing."

"Is this an interview?"

"Off the record," he says.

"You and I both know there's no such thing as off the record." This time the smile she flashes him is whole and bright. He could get used to her smiling at him like that.

CHAPTER 10

Over the next three months, Jimmy and Brett meet regularly at the bar across from the old bank building. Sometimes they meet during Brett's thirty-minute lunch break. Sometimes it's at night, after her shift ends, which Jimmy prefers because they don't have to rush that way. Regardless of the time, Jimmy always orders a beer, and Brett always orders a Coke. They share a basket of fries and talk about the investigation without actually talking about the investigation. She tells him nothing that he doesn't already know, nothing Detective Rausch hasn't already stated in his useless press conferences. But Jimmy doesn't push her. He wants to know what's happening with the case, but not at the expense of their newly budding friendship.

One cold and damp evening in the middle of March, Brett bursts into the bar along with a gust of wind and sideways rain. She shakes water from her jacket and sinks into what Jimmy has started calling their confessional. It's the same corner booth where he first learned her name. Raindrops glisten on her cheeks, but she doesn't bother to brush them away. For the first time since they started meeting like this, she orders a beer.

"Rough day?" Jimmy asks.

She keeps her lips pinched tight as she shakes her head.

Only after the beer arrives, after she's taken a long drink from the glass, does she speak. "It's so goddamn frustrating. Every tip I bring to Rausch, he slaps down. I feel like I'm over there beating my head against a brick wall. What's the point of having a tip line if you aren't going to follow up on the tips?"

She looks across the table, her eyes searching for something. "Where's Trixie?"

"I have to leave her in the car now," Jimmy says. "Last time we were here, she tried to eat someone else's hamburger."

Brett laughs and takes another drink of beer. Jimmy waits a few minutes until she looks more relaxed before bringing up the investigation again.

"What kind of tips is Rausch ignoring?" He doesn't think she'll answer. She's always brushed him off before.

Jimmy doesn't know what's different about today, if the weather is making her restless, or if the case has been dragging on too long for her liking, or if she's just reached a breaking point with Rausch. She says, "This girl called a few weeks ago. She told me she tried to talk to someone last year after Cherish was in the news, but no one ever called her back. She goes to Willamette. Lives in a house with some other girls. She said that last June, they kept seeing this dark blue sedan. It would drive by their house late at night. Sometimes it would park outside and idle there for hours before driving away again."

"They didn't call the police when they saw it out there?"

"The first time it happened, no, because they didn't really think it was a big deal. The second time the girls called their boyfriends. The boys came over with baseball bats and flashlights and their big hulking jock bodies and chased the car away. But it came back a third time, and that's when they were really spooked. They turned off all the lights, locked the doors, and huddled together in the living room with kitchen knives. Of course, they should have called the cops, but they didn't. Because they're young and stupid and think they're invincible. Now Rausch is using that as an excuse not to follow up. He says they're just trying to get attention."

Her face pinches with anger that she's trying to keep tucked away. "If someone had listened to them last year, the first time, they could have increased patrols in the area, or, I don't know, sent out a bulletin with the description of the car. Of course, 'dark blue sedan' doesn't narrow things down very much, does it?"

"But it's better than nothing," they say at the same time.

She smiles, but there is no energy to it. She gestures to Jimmy's half-empty pint glass. "Want another? I'm buying."

A few minutes later, she returns to their table with full and frothing pints.

"The creepiest part—" She sits back down, splashing a little beer over the side of her glass. "They said that the only reason they even noticed someone out there was because they could see him smoking. They would look out their window and see the cherry ember glow of a cigarette. It would flare hot for a second, then fade, then flare."

Jimmy's chest pinched as he thought about Cherish's roommates and the man they saw smoking outside their house in the days before Cherish's murder.

"Where is it?" he asks.

"What? Their house?"

He nods. Brett tells him and asks if he's going to go out there.

"I might. Seems like it could be something worth checking out."

There's a satisfied look in her eyes like she was hoping this would be the outcome. "There's another one," she says, leaning forward with her elbows on the table. "The coach for the OSU girls' soccer team caught a man lurking in the locker room during practice. She went after him, got a few hits in, but he managed to slip her grasp somehow."

"Certainly that's something Rausch would be interested in."

"You'd think." Her jaw tightens. So do her fists. "He laughed and said the girls' should take it as a compliment and that the coach should mind her own business. He said the guy we're looking for wouldn't be so brazen, that this was probably some pervy liberal arts teacher trying to get his rocks off. Harmless. That's what he said. Harmless." The second time she says the word, she spits it out like a bitter seed. "Like the first girl, this coach said she called last year, but no one followed up. Jimmy, both of these calls came in before Natasha was killed. "

Her hands encircle the pint glass on the table in front of her. Since she brought it over, she hasn't taken a single sip.

"I keep thinking if I'd been the one to take those calls, if I knew about them, maybe I could have done something, you know? Maybe I could have stopped him before he got to Natasha." Her voice trembles.

"Hey." Jimmy reaches across the table and lays his hand on Brett's arm. "It might not have made a difference, you know? Even if you had been able to follow up on those tips? They still might not have led you to him in time."

She moves her arm out from under his grasp. "Thanks, but I'm not asking you to try and make me feel better about this."

"Then what are you asking me to do?" Jimmy pulls his hand back, the words coming out more sharply than he intended.

"The Roach is fumbling this case. He's focused on the wrong things, and if someone doesn't point him in a different direction, in a few months, we're all going to have another dead girl on our hands." She leans toward him. "I've read every single article you've written about Cherish and Natasha. I know about your research into other cases, too, about your theories that the Ophelia Killer has killed more than just the five women we're focused on in Salem. They talk about you in meetings. Hell, Rausch even has you at the top of his suspect list."

"You could probably get fired for telling me that," Jimmy says.

"Probably, but I'm willing to take that risk if it means catching the real killer before he takes another girl."

"Rausch could be right about me, you know."

Brett snorts a laugh. "Sure, he could."

"Why is this so important to you?" He can see something simmering behind the obvious disappointment and frustration of working with someone as incompetent as Detective Rausch.

She shakes her head. "I don't want anyone else getting hurt."

"It seems like it's something more personal than that, too," he presses her.

"I should go. I'm meeting friends." She fumbles in her pocket for cash to pay for their fries and beers.

"I can get it," Jimmy says, but she ignores him, lays the money on the table, and slides out of the booth.

It's only after he follows her out to the parking lot, when they're standing beneath the awning of the bar, pulling on their coats, and trying to decide if there's going to be a break in the rain, that she tells him the truth.

"You're right, you know," she says. "It is personal."

White clouds of breath overlap and disappear above their heads.

"When I was fourteen..." She speaks so quietly Jimmy has to lean in to hear her even though they're already standing shoulder to shoulder.

"When I was fourteen, my older sister was murdered. Her body was found in the woods near my grandparents' house in Washington. The police." She pauses to take a deep breath, and her face tilts toward the sky, a black and endless void. "They were pretty much useless. I don't remember much, but Rausch reminds me of the idiots investigating my sister's case. I became a cop because I didn't want anyone else's family to go through what my family went through, and now—" She cuts herself off and shakes her head like she's trying to clear away unwanted memories. "I don't want another girl to die, that's all. It doesn't seem like too much to ask."

"It's not." Jimmy squeezes her elbow gently. "I'll talk to the girl who saw the car and to the soccer coach and see what I can find out from them. We still have five months, Bretty. There's still time to catch this guy."

She tilts her head to look at him, a furrow forming between her eyebrows. "What did you call me?"

The nickname just slipped out. Jimmy doesn't even know where it came from. His cheeks burn, and he's grateful they're standing outside where she can't see how completely embarrassed he is.

"Sorry," he stammers. "I don't know what—I didn't think—"

"It's fine," she says, resting her hand on his arm. "Most of the time, people just call me Brett or Buchanan. But, sometimes it's 'hey, bitch.' So, Bretty is at least better than that. Actually, I think I kind of like it. Only from you, though." Then she turns her focus onto the zipper of her coat, struggling to get it closed. "I have to stop coming here. These fries aren't doing me any favors."

"You could always order the salad next time?" He's trying to make her laugh again, to smile at least. He's been at this longer than she has and knows how easily this work of chasing monsters can leave you brittle and shattered. You have to find outlets, figure out a way to find some good, some humanity, even in the face of all this death. You have to cling to the parts of you that are soft and kind. Like humor. Like laughter.

A smile trembles on her lips, though it doesn't make it to her eyes. Then she says, "Come for a run with me? Tomorrow morning. Meet me at Lake Wirth at sunrise. Bring Trixie. You work off the beer. I'll work off these fries."

He says yes, even though he's not a runner. He will say yes to anything if it means spending more time with her. Plus, he wants to find out more about her sister. Maybe he can dig up more information about what happened with the investigation, where it went wrong, why it stalled. Maybe he can even bring Brett and her family some small amount of closure.

After agreeing on a time to meet the following day, Jimmy ducks out from beneath the awning first. He waves over his shoulder as he races to the car, where Trixie waits with her nose pressed to the glass.

CHAPTER 11

Two months later and five pounds lighter, Jimmy finally has something to show Brett. They've been meeting at Lake Wirth three days a week to run, rain or shine, since the middle of March. Jimmy hasn't gotten much faster with all that practice, but Brett has. She and Trixie often speed ahead of him, chasing down the dirt path that circles the lake, growing smaller as they move farther away.

As April becomes May, the weather turns from fog and damp to bright and warm. Flowers bloom, trees blossom, Jimmy's allergies start acting up, but he and Trixie still meet up with Brett every Monday, Wednesday, and Friday morning. They part ways after every run. Jimmy goes home to shower, change, and feed Trixie breakfast before heading to the press room. He assumes Brett does something similar, ending up at the offices where Rausch's special unit is still spinning its wheels.

Finally, with three weeks in May already gone, Jimmy asks Brett to come over to his apartment after work rather than meet up at the bar. She gives him a curious look but says she'll be there around six. He spends the rest of the day nervously preparing. He cleans the apartment and burns a sheet pan of tater tots, which means he has to buy more from the store. By some luck, he doesn't burn the second batch. When Brett arrives at his apartment, Jimmy has already opened a bottle of wine, drank a glass, and is feeling more relaxed.

Brett greets Trixie with a hearty scratch behind the ears, then she holds out a carton of butter pecan ice cream. "I brought dessert."

He puts the ice cream in the freezer and offers her a glass of wine. When he hands her the glass, he gestures to the table where the file waits. He skips the small talk and cuts straight to the point. "I called in a favor with a friend who was able to get a copy of your sister's case from the Crestwood Police Department."

Brett brushes her fingers over the single folder lying on the table. "Is this it? It's pretty thin."

Too thin. When Jimmy told Annabeth he needed everything she could get on a seventeen-year-old case from a small police department in northern Washington, he thought it would take a few weeks. She called after only three days to tell him the Crestwood police had sent over less than thirty pages of information. He must have sounded disappointed because she rushed to add that she'd double-checked, triple-checked, asked if there wasn't something else, some other place the file might be hiding? But no, the Crestwood receptionist said that, except for the physical evidence which would obviously remain with the department, everything Jimmy got is everything the Crestwood police have on file for Margot Buchanan.

"Is this a joke?" Brett says, opening the folder and scanning the top sheet.

He slaps the folder closed. "Are you sure you want to do this? There's no going back once you crack this open. You won't be able to unsee the things that are in here."

"Are there pictures?"

"A few." They're poor black-and-white photocopies but detailed enough to give a person nightmares.

But the pictures aren't what Jimmy's worried about. He read

through the notes the second they landed on his desk. Though there aren't as many as he'd hoped, they're still gruesome enough to shatter her. According to the file, Brett was only thirteen when her older sister was murdered. Almost fourteen, when Brett's telling the story. Too young, either way, Jimmy thinks. What she remembers from that time, what she's told Jimmy when they've talked about it, is a watered-down version of the truth. Her understanding of events is basically whatever her grandparents told her and whatever she's been able to find in newspaper archives since then, which isn't very much.

Margot Buchanan went missing in August of 1964. Police were notified. The town looked for her. A few days later, they found her body in a wooded area. The detective told Brett's parents that Margot had been murdered. The official cause of death was blunt force trauma. The police didn't tell them anything else. At least, Brett told Jimmy, she was never told anything else.

Your sister is dead. Someone killed her. That's all her parents told her about the matter. And when she asked questions, they told her they didn't know anything else and started crying. So what Brett knows now about the case, what she's told Jimmy about it, is even less than what's inside this too-thin file folder. He knows from reading through it already that this small stack of pages will change her life forever. They will rewrite her history.

Brett pulls her hand away from the folder. Her shoulders stiffen as if she's steeling herself for what she's about to see. She takes a drink of wine, then looks at Jimmy and nods. Jimmy lifts his hand, giving her full access.

Brett pulls a chair out from the table, sits down, and slides the folder close to her. She spends a moment staring at the cover before finally opening it. Jimmy sits in a chair across from her, watching silently as she reads through every jotted note and typed report. She twists her wine glass by the stem but doesn't drink. When she gets to the pictures, the small muscle in her jaw tightens. Her finger hovers a moment over the photograph, and then she slowly closes the folder. Her eyes close, too, and Jimmy can't tell if she's about to cry or scream or laugh. Finally, she flutters her eyes open again, lifts the wine glass, drains it in one drink, and holds it out to Jimmy.

"You got anything stronger than this?" Her voice is hoarse.

Jimmy rummages in the cupboard above the fridge for the whiskey he never drinks. He hasn't touched it since he poured a glass for Detective Rausch last July. He pours two glasses now, one for Brett, one for himself, and adds a single ice cube to both. Trixie, who was sleeping under the table and got up when he did, bumps against his leg. He takes an ice cube from the tray and drops it on the floor for her. She noses it across the linoleum, her tail wagging happily.

Jimmy sets the whiskey in front of Brett. She throws the shot back and makes a face.

"Want more?" Jimmy asks.

The chair scrapes across the floor as she gets up, grabs the bottle off the counter, and sits back down. She pours more whiskey into her glass, but this time drinks slowly, clinking the ice in a circle. She hasn't said anything since she asked for a drink, and Jimmy is starting to worry she won't say anything about what she read in the file at all. But he doesn't want to push her.

He sips his whiskey, which is too strong for him even with an ice cube, but he doesn't get up to water it down because he doesn't want to move or blink or even breathe until she says something. *Say something, say anything*, he sends the command to her silently, until finally she takes a deep breath and exhales loudly.

With breathless, broken-hearted realization, she says, "Margot was dead before we even started looking for her."

It wasn't what he expected her to say, not what he thought she'd notice first. He thought she would be upset about the fact that seventeen years ago, the police had a suspect in their grasp but no evidence to bring him in. A kid named Danny Cyrus, who Margot was apparently flirting with that summer.

Jimmy thought Brett would be upset, too, about the incompetence of the detective, Stan Harcourt, and how little he did in the way of an actual investigation. But no, it's the coroner's report she latches on to, the probable time of death, the days her sister spent decomposing in the forest before anyone found her.

"I've spent half my life thinking that if I had just told someone sooner, done something sooner, that she might still be alive." Brett's voice is thick with emotion. "I've spent half my life thinking I could have saved her. What a waste of time."

She tips the whiskey to her lips and drains the glass. A shudder rolls through her, then she flips through the folder a second time, slower now, squinting at each detail. She stops at one of the pictures of her sister lying on her back in a dappled wood.

Brett's eyes glisten, and her mouth pinches into a frown. She shakes her head and flips the page to a written report describing the items found with Margot's body. By some miracle, she was still partly dressed in her bra and underwear, with no signs of sexual assault. She clutched a bouquet of wildflowers to her breasts. Her hair was tangled with leaves and more flowers. Her tongue had been cut from her mouth.

"It can't be a coincidence, right?" Brett asks, the trembling emotion in her voice now sharpening to a hard edge. "Was he there? The man we're looking for now, the Ophelia Killer? Did he kill Margot? Is that what I'm looking at here?"

Before Jimmy can respond, Brett starts rattling off the similarities, and he nods along, agreeing with everything she says.

There are too many things the same for Margot's case not to be linked to the Ophelia Killer. Jimmy has always wondered if there were more than the eleven he's sure about, if there were women killed before 1967, murders that went unnoticed, others like Margot who have stayed lost in the cold case files of their local departments, moldering away in dank basements for who knows how many decades. It's a lucky break, finding Margot's case. Jimmy feels like he should say something about destiny, about the rise and fall of fates, their paths converging to hunt down a killer who never should have wandered free for so long.

Instead, he says, "Are you hungry? I made tater tots."

She gives him a baffled look and flips the folder closed again. This time she keeps her hand pressed flat on top of it. "Someone has to tell Rausch about this. The sooner, the better."

She scoots the chair back and starts to get up, taking the folder with her.

"Not you." Jimmy snatches the folder from her grasp.

Trixie, excited by their movements, gets up from her spot underneath the table and winds around their legs.

"Someone has to go up there." Brett reaches for the folder, but Jimmy pulls it away. "Someone has to go back and talk to the detective who investigated her case. Talk to the people who were in Crestwood that summer. Maybe someone will remember something."

"Yes, but that someone is not going to be you," Jimmy repeats, emphasizing the words. "If Rausch finds out you were looking at this file, you could get fired. At the very least, you'll get reassigned back down to patrol duty. They'll certainly kick you off this investigation."

She works her lips between her teeth, and Jimmy realizes with a jolt that he knows her well enough now to recognize she's scared.

"Then you have to take it to him," she says.

"I want to go up there first."

"What? No. Jimmy, this is bigger than your stupid story."

He bristles at her words. "I'm doing this for you, Brett. Don't forget that."

"If you were doing it for me, you'd take the file to Rausch."

"So he can ignore it like he's ignored everything else?"

Brett sighs and sinks into the chair. She reaches to pet Trixie, who's leaning against the side of her leg, blinking up at her with woeful brown eyes.

Jimmy sighs, too, but doesn't sit down. He keeps the folder tucked under his arm as he talks. "I followed up on those tips, too, Brett. The ones Rausch told you not to bother with?"

She looks at him with a spark of hope in her eyes. "And?"

"The girls were pretty much dead-ends. They couldn't come up with much beyond a dark blue sedan. One of them thought there was a Z in the license plate, but the other said she thought it was 2. So, that didn't go anywhere."

The spark fades.

"The soccer coach, though, had a lot to tell me about the man she saw. She described him to me in pretty good detail. Mid-thirties, she guessed, dark blond hair that curled around the collar of the security guard jacket he was wearing. She said his eyes were blue and cold, that he had a strange look on his face, angry but also bemused. Those were her words. She said he looked like a tiger who'd been torturing a mouse. I had her talk to a sketch artist. They came up with a sketch. She says it's a pretty good likeness. I took the sketch to the Oregon State campus security office, but they said they didn't have anyone working for them who looked like the man in the sketch."

"So, he's posing as a security guard? That's how he can get close enough to take the girls?"

"Probably. But there's still the possibility that the man in the locker room isn't the man we're looking for."

"Show me the sketch," Brett says.

Jimmy's been carrying a copy in his back pocket since the artist drew it up three weeks ago. He takes it out now and hands it to her. She unfolds the paper, studies it a moment, then shakes her head.

"I've never seen him before."

"But someone in Crestwood might recognize him. If this man and the man who killed Cherish and Natasha is the same as the man who killed your sister—"

"Jimmy, I'm sorry." She's on her feet again, gripping the black-and-white sketch tightly. "I know you don't want to tell Rausch about this, but he needs to know. This could be it. This could be the break we've been hoping for. It's the end of May, but as long as the Ophelia Killer sticks to his previous timeline, that still leaves us two months. We have time to stop him, Jimmy, but you can't do it by yourself."

"I know." He takes the picture from her, folds it, and puts it back in his pocket. "But let me take it to Rausch, okay? You stay out of it. I'll tell him everything, and I'll tell him he has to send someone up to Crestwood."

She nods, agreeing, then asks, "What if he doesn't listen to you?"

"Then I'll go up to Crestwood myself." He smiles, trying to reassure her. "One way or the other, we're catching this bastard before he kills another girl."

Brett drops her hand and scratches Trixie's ears. Her gaze is unfocused as she stares across the room. Trixie's tongue lolls out the side of her mouth in pure happiness. After a few seconds, Brett shifts her gaze back to Jimmy and says, "I think I'm ready for those tater tots, now, if you're still offering."

CHAPTER 12

The day after showing Brett her sister's file, Jimmy comes home during his lunch break to walk Trixie and finds his apartment door standing open. From somewhere inside, he can hear Trixie's muffled barks. Anger and panic flares in his chest. He hesitates outside the door, slowing his breathing, steadying his shaking hands, wishing he was the kind of man who carried a gun.

All of the neighbors' doors are closed. He's never home long enough to get to know them anyway, but certainly, one of them would let him use their phone to call the police. From inside his apartment comes a muffled thump and the sound of someone rifling through drawers. A shadow flashes across the doorway, then another. A male voice thunders, "Jesus, how many pens does this guy need?"

"You're not here to count pens, Fred."

Jimmy recognizes the second man's voice immediately, and his anger flares hotter, fueled by the fear he no longer feels. He steps over the threshold into his apartment.

The three uniformed officers moving through the small space is overkill. They keep tripping over one another and bumping elbows. Jimmy recognizes one guy as the bumbling Clodfelter from Cherish Spalding's crime scene.

Clodfelter flaps his hands at another man with short red hair and says, "I already looked over there."

Detective Michael Rausch stands apart from it all in the kitchen. He's facing away from the commotion, staring through the balcony door at the duck pond. Trixie is locked out on the balcony, presumably by Rausch. Her breath fogs up the glass with each demanding bark to be let back inside, but the detective ignores her. His fingers are laced behind his back, and he taps one thumb in a slow rhythm.

It takes Jimmy four long strides to get to the kitchen. One officer sees him, and his mouth hinges open, but he doesn't say anything or try to stop him.

"What the hell do you think you're doing?" Jimmy shoves Rausch to one side and reaches to open the balcony door.

Rausch lays a hand on Jimmy's arm, stopping him. "She'll only be in the way."

"No, she won't." Jimmy wrenches his arm back. "Because you're all leaving."

A smug, self-satisfied smile creeps onto Rausch's face as he pulls a folded piece of paper from his jacket pocket and holds it out to Jimmy. "We'll leave when we're good and ready to leave. And I'm only going to ask you once to not interfere. I'd hate to have to arrest you for obstruction."

Jimmy snatches the paper from Rausch and scans the fine print, trying to figure out what kind of lies the detective told a judge to get him to sign off on this ridiculous search. He shoves the paper back into Rausch's hands. "You know you're wasting your time, right?"

"We'll see." He gestures to the kitchen table. "They're almost finished. Why don't you and I sit down and have a little chat."

"I have nothing to say to you." He grabs Trixie's leash hanging by the front door, returns to the kitchen, slides open the balcony door, and kneels down beside her. She leaps at him, licking his face. He clips the leash to her collar and brings her inside.

Rausch stands to one side but never takes his eyes off Jimmy.

In the living room, something crashes to the floor. Trixie starts barking again. Jimmy hushes her and turns to Rausch. "Are you going to pay for whatever they break?"

Rausch snorts a half-laugh. He takes a pack of cigarettes out of his pocket.

"Don't smoke in here," Jimmy warns him.

Rausch shrugs. He pulls a cigarette out of the pack but doesn't light it, just flips it in his fingers, rolling the paper over his knuckles. "I've been working back over the timeline," he says. "It all fits."

"What are you talking about?"

"You move back to the area. Bam. Girls start showing up dead. Then you start showing up to my crime scenes, inserting yourself into the investigation, taking a particular interest in certain girls and not others."

"I take an interest in the ones that are similar," Jimmy says, trying to keep his voice level. He doesn't want to come off sounding defensive because he knows how Rausch could use that against him. But he can't stand here and say nothing either. "We're on the same side, Rausch. We both want the same thing."

"I'm not so sure about that anymore." Rausch drops the unlit cigarette back into his pocket.

He leaves the kitchen to go stand in front of the living room wall. Jimmy follows him, tugging on Trixie's leash to get her to come along. Her tail is tucked between her legs. A low growl rolls through her chest as she eyes the three officers darting around the apartment, opening drawers and lifting cushions.

Several things have been added to Jimmy's wall since Rausch was in his apartment last July. Natasha Tinneford's picture, for one. Plus, a description of the car the sorority girls saw parked on their street. And a copy of the sketch of the man the soccer coach confronted in her locker room. Rausch takes the drawing down and holds it up to the light. His eyes flick back and forth between the picture and Jimmy's face as if he's comparing the two.

"Is this our guy?" he finally asks.

"Could be."

"And what information did you base this sketch off of?"

"There was a witness—"

"Bullshit." Rausch spits the word out then crumples the paper in his fist. "There are no witnesses."

Jimmy draws Trixie's leash a little tighter. She presses her warm body against his legs. "There's a soccer coach at Oregon State who says she caught a man lurking in the girls' locker room. Based on her description, that's what the guy she saw looked like."

Rausch tries to smooth out the paper again. He frowns at the sketch, then glares at Jimmy. "This could be anyone. Or no one. This could be you trying to steer us in the wrong direction, so you can choose your next victim."

"Like I told you the last time you were here," Jimmy says through gritted teeth. "If you have proof, go ahead and arrest me already. But I'm telling you, the man we're looking for would never be so brazen as to hang out with cops the way I do. He certainly wouldn't help them. What he does to these women, the kind of relationship he believes he has with them, it's a private one."

The man they're hunting wouldn't be so blatant about hanging his victims' pictures on his wall. He wouldn't pal around with cops. He wouldn't write articles. He would sit in a quiet, dark room with the cut-out tongues, listening to their whispered secrets, keeping the women all to himself.

One of the officers pops his head out of the bedroom door and says, "I think we may have found something."

An arrogant spark flashes in the detective's eyes as he spins away from Jimmy and strides into the bedroom.

Jimmy trails after him, and even though he knows he's innocent, knows there's nothing to find that could mark him as a killer, his heart starts to race. He doesn't trust Rausch not to twist facts to make them fit this bullshit story he's made up about Jimmy's involvement in this case.

Apprehension turns to dread when he steps into the bedroom to find Detective Rausch flipping through Margot Buchanan's case file. The very same file Jimmy was planning to bring to Rausch as a possible lead looks damning in this cramped and dimly lit space.

Between Rausch and the three officers, there's barely any room left for Jimmy to step through the doorway. A bead of sweat trickles down his back and cools against his skin, shivering a chill up his spine.

"What am I looking at here?" Rausch frowns and waves the folder in the air.

"I was going to bring that to your office next week, after the holiday." Even if Rausch decided to work on Memorial Day, it's still a good excuse for why Jimmy didn't bring the file in as soon as he realized the possible connection between the cases. It's better than the truth, anyway.

Part of the reason Jimmy held off showing Rausch the Buchanan file sooner is pure selfishness. He wanted to show Brett first, and he wanted to take the story to Tadd, so maybe he deserves what's happening now. But the other reason he didn't go to Rausch right away is because he knew exactly what Rausch's response would be, and he's sick of wasting time.

Detective Rausch slaps Margot's case file closed, and a blast of laughter escapes his lips. "You're kidding me with this, right? Who did you have to sweet talk to get this file? Oh, and let me guess, you think this seventeen-year-old case is connected."

"I think if you take a closer look at it, you'll see the similarities, too."

Rausch hands the file to one of the officers. "Bag this."

Jimmy starts to protest, but Rausch cuts him off, swinging his hand in the air over his head. "And bag up all that stuff in the living room, too. That shrine he's built for the girls he's killed."

"It's not a shrine."

"I don't give a shit what you call it. It's evidence, and I'm taking it with me."

The officers slide out of the bedroom and begin pulling everything off the wall. Jimmy grits his teeth as every scrap, every piece he worked so hard to find, is taken down and stuffed into cardboard boxes.

"You're wasting your time on me, Rausch," Jimmy says. "The real killer's out there right now hunting his next victim. Every minute you spend trying to make me look guilty is another minute you're giving him to get away with murder."

"You're making this harder on yourself, Slim-Jim. You know that, right? All you have to do is tell me the truth."

"You need to send someone to Crestwood," Jimmy says.

Rausch tilts his head to one side. "You ever been to Crestwood, Slim-Jim?"

"I've never even heard of Crestwood before I saw that file."

The last scrap of paper is taken off the wall. The officer drops the lid on the box and straightens.

"That's it, Mikey," he says, talking to Detective Rausch. "Want us to take him in, too?"

The detective's expression is hard to read—calm, but there's a spark in his eyes, the flash of something deadly. He pops his knuckles, then he shakes his head. "Let's give him a night to think things over. He's not going anywhere. Isn't that right, Slim-Jim? Because you know how that would look, don't you? If you left town right now? Don't worry, he'll still be here in the morning. We can come back for him then, after we make it official."

The three officers leave the apartment with the box.

Detective Rausch stops in the doorway, turns to Jimmy, and says, "You can make this easier on yourself, you know. Come down to the station with me right now, come clean. I can help you out here, Jimmy. I can make your life easy, or I can make it hell. The choice is yours."

He waits with his hand on the doorknob.

Jimmy counts the seconds as the silence stretches between them. Rausch is bluffing. If he had any good evidence at all, Jimmy would already be in handcuffs.

Twenty seconds pass before Rausch shakes his head, disappointed. "Well, if you change your mind, you know where to find me."

The door slams shut, rattling the pictures hanging on the wall. Jimmy locks the deadbolt, then bends over and unclips the leash from Trixie's collar.

She bumps against him, sticking close to his heels as he moves through the apartment, pulling a duffel bag from the closet, stuffing it with clothes and toiletries, enough for a couple of nights. He moves into the kitchen to start packing some food for Trixie but hesitates, wondering if he should leave her behind, and ask Brett to come over and stay with her. There's no time for that. He should have left for Crestwood the day he read through Margot Buchanan's file, the second he realized what he'd found.

Rausch was never going to be helpful. Jimmy knew that from the beginning, but he didn't think the man would be so completely arrogant that he would ignore what so obviously needed to be done next and fixate on Jimmy instead.

The phone hanging on the kitchen wall jangles Jimmy from his single-minded panic. He answers with a frustrated, "What?"

"Jimmy? What the hell is going on?" His editor sounds furious, but beneath that is a layer of fear and of relief, too. "You left for lunch and never came back. Then this bumbling oaf of a detective bursts into my office asking all sorts of bullshit questions about you. What have you gotten yourself caught up in? Jimmy? Are you there?"

"I'm here. I'm sorry, Tadd. I don't really have time to talk right now."

"Well, you better make the time, buddy, because I did you a favor today that could get me fired, so at the very least, you owe me a goddamn explanation."

Jimmy sighs. "Meet me at O'Shanty's in ten minutes."

It will take Jimmy five minutes to get to the pub down the street from the *Statesman Journal*. He spends the other five packing Trixie's things and turning off the lights in his apartment. Trixie's tail wags uncontrollably when she realizes she's coming along.

"Don't get your hopes up, girl," Jimmy mutters to her as they step into the hall. He locks the door behind them.

CHAPTER 13

Before Jimmy has a chance to settle onto the stool beside Tadd, the bartender sets a beer in front of him.

"I didn't order that," Jimmy says.

"I ordered it for you," Tadd says. "And I'm glad I did because you look like shit, my friend. Shit that got run over by a train. Maybe I should have ordered us shots instead."

"I can't. I'm driving." Jimmy takes a sip of beer.

Tadd nods his approval and says, "You gonna tell me where you're headed?"

"Remember I told you about that possible lead up in Washington, right?"

Tadd nods again and gestures for the bartender to bring them two more beers.

"I'm serious, Tadd. This one beer's enough. My car's packed, and Trixie's waiting. As soon as I'm done here, we're headed north."

Tadd gives Jimmy a long look. "Do you know what that cop said to me?"

"I can take a guess."

"He thinks you killed those girls, Jimmy."

The bartender stiffens and gives them a look that's hard to read. Jimmy can't tell if he wants to know more or kick them out. When the bartender catches Jimmy watching him, he looks away and busies himself with stacking pint glasses. O'Shanty's is the kind of bar where people show up after all the other bars close down for the night. It's barely two in the afternoon. Jimmy and Tadd are the only customers here right now.

"He thinks you're the Ophelia Killer," Tadd says.

"What do you think?"

"He's a blustering windbag full of shit, obviously. I don't know how he can even see anything with his head so far up his own ass the way it is. But what I think doesn't really matter, does it? It's how he spins the story. You and I both know that plenty of innocent men have gone to jail based on less evidence than what he claims to have on you."

"It's circumstantial," Jimmy says. "No, it's not even that. It's nothing. He has nothing. Because there is nothing. He would have arrested me if he had anything more than bullshit." Jimmy drains the rest of his beer and slams the empty glass on the bar top with frustration. "I feel crazy. Tell me I'm not crazy."

"You know I can't do that." Tadd laughs. "You gotta be a certain kind of crazy to do this work."

Tadd nudges the second glass of beer in Jimmy's direction. Jimmy pulls it close but doesn't drink. He hunches over it, watching the bubbles rise to the surface and pop.

"How did you do it for so long?" he asks.

Before he was promoted to editor, Tadd worked the crime beat. He spent over a decade rooting out man's darkest sins and turning them into half-page articles.

"How did you stare so long into the abyss and not lose your mind?"

"What makes you think I didn't?" Tadd takes a drink, then

says, "I miss it sometimes, you know. What? That surprises you? It's true. Sometimes I think I'd like to give up this editor gig and go back to rolling around in the mud with the rest of you."

"Sure, you think that," Jimmy says. "Until you find yourself staring down at a dead girl with her tongue cut out."

Tadd winces.

"If we don't find this guy, it's going to happen again. I don't think I can do it. I don't think I can bury another one."

"Then don't."

Jimmy shakes his head. "It's not that simple."

"Of course it's that simple." Tadd shifts his weight on the barstool, turning so his body is angled toward Jimmy. "Look, it's true. You see a lot of terrible shit when you're working stories like the ones you chase. And you can let it crush you, or you can turn it into something good. Think about it. You are the only one who can tell the story, the true version. The cops won't. They'll always have their own agenda. You're learning that the hard way right now. But the family sure as hell won't tell the truth either. They'll leave things out, intentionally or otherwise. They'll always say the victim was perfect. No one's perfect. Remember that. But what you can do, what we do, is show them everything. We tell the whole goddamn truth and nothing but the truth. The good parts, the terrible parts, the parts no one else cares about. We get all these jumbled pieces, and we fit them together until it makes sense. You think you know where to find this guy?"

"I think I know where to start looking."

"Then what the hell are you waiting for?"

Jimmy turns the pint glass. More bubbles rise. "What if my hunch is wrong? What if I'm letting my personal feelings get in the way of the truth?"

"Is that what you think is happening?"

Jimmy stares at his reflection in the mirror hanging behind the bar. The glass is cracked and distorted, making him look ten years older. He might be chasing the wrong story, chasing his feelings for Brett straight into a dead-end, but his gut tells him otherwise.

"Jimmy, my boy, you're in too deep to slow down now," Tadd says. "That detective who came by the office this afternoon wasn't messing around. I bought you a few days, sure, but he'll be back, and the next time he comes around, he'll find whatever it is he's hoping to find, even if he has to make it up as he goes along. If you're onto something with this Crestwood lead, if you think it might be enough to get him off your back once and for all, then there's really no decision to be made here, is there?"

Tadd's right. Jimmy has to go. If there are answers in Crestwood, he needs to find them now before Detective Rausch convinces the county prosecutor that behind Jimmy's pen and a stack of papers lurks a monster.

"You think you can get this story wrapped and ready by Sunday?" Tadd claps Jimmy on the shoulder.

"Ha, very funny."

"What makes you think I'm kidding? Two days seems plenty long enough to me." But Tadd flashes Jimmy a toothy smile and gestures to the full pint of beer still sitting in front of him. "You sure I can't talk you into another one for the road?"

Jimmy drops a couple of dollars on the bar and waves to Tadd on his way out.

Five and a half hours later, after one stop to fill up on gas and two stops to pee on the side of the road, Jimmy and Trixie pull into the parking lot of a roadside motel on the southern edge of Crestwood, Washington. He leaves Trixie in the car to ask about room availability.

The motel manager smiles warmly at him and says he's in luck. "We've got one room left at the end."

He asks about the pet policy.

"Dogs are fine. Bears have to sleep outside." She hands him a room key with a playful wink. "You sure are lucky, you know that? I tell you, if you'd come even a few minutes later, chances are you'd be sleeping in your car tonight. The Memorial Day Holiday always draws a good-sized crowd. What better way to kick off summer than whale watching tours, fireworks shows, crab cookouts, and Mary's fresh-baked apple pies? Are you planning on staying the whole weekend or just tonight?"

Jimmy isn't sure how to answer since so much depends on how quickly he finds what he's looking for. He says, "Let's start with two nights," and hopes it'll be more than enough.

It's almost eight o'clock at night, too late to do much of anything as far as an investigation goes. But Jimmy feels the press of time and doesn't want to waste a single minute. He takes the sketch of the man he believes to be the Ophelia Killer from his back pocket and slides it in front of the manager. It's the copy he showed Brett last night. It's sheer luck he wore the same pair of jeans today, and luck, too, that Detective Rausch only searched his apartment but left his person alone.

"Have you ever seen this man before?" Jimmy asks.

The manager perches a pair of reading glasses on the end of her nose and squints closely at the picture. She shakes her head. "Can't say I have. Friend of yours?"

"Just someone I'm looking for," he says.

The manager takes her glasses off. Her shoulders are stiff. She's no longer smiling. Something has changed in how she perceives Jimmy. He's no longer a harmless tourist to welcome and coddle. He's here for something else. Something she doesn't want to be involved in. Her hand inches toward the motel room key still sitting on the counter between them, and he can see it in her eyes that she's about to tell him to keep driving.

He flashes a smile, hoping to soften her again, and snatches the key out of her grasp. "He's a friend of a friend," he says, stretching the truth. "She's got something of his she wants to give back. Last she knew, he was hanging around Crestwood. I'm hoping someone around here might recognize him and point me in the right direction."

"I'm afraid I don't know anyone who looks like that." She's still suspicious of him, but less so now.

"That's fine." He keeps smiling at her. "You mind telling me where I can find the police station?"

Her frown deepens again. She jerks her thumb at the wall behind her. "Two miles that way."

They're not very good directions, but Jimmy thanks her anyway.

With a grunt, the woman goes back to flipping through a home and garden magazine, all the charm gone from her voice when she says, "Enjoy your stay."

Jimmy drops his suitcase in the room. He clips on Trixie's leash and walks her around outside the motel for a few minutes, giving her a chance to sniff and do her business. When he brings her into the room, she sniffs a few minutes more before settling onto the carpet beside the bed with a loud sigh. Jimmy scratches her head and gives her a dog biscuit. As she crunches her way through the treat, Jimmy picks up the phone sitting on the nightstand and dials Brett's number.

She picks up after three rings.

"Hey, Bretty."

"Jimmy? What did you say to Rausch? He's losing his damn mind. He's been locked in his office all afternoon, screaming into the phone, trying to get the prosecutor to charge you with murder.

You were supposed to show him the file, Jimmy. You were supposed to—"

"Brett. Shut up a minute and let me talk. I showed him the file. And it didn't do a damn thing to change his mind."

"So, what now? You have to go up there, right? You have to go to Crestwood."

"I'm already here. I drove up right after he was done trashing my apartment."

She falls silent. Then he hears the smallest of sighs. "Oh, Jimmy, I hope you know what you're doing."

"Luck's been on my side so far, and if it keeps up, I'll be back before Rausch even knows I'm gone, but can you do something for me? Can you keep him distracted? Bug him about those tips you gave me again. Try to get him pointed in the right direction."

"You know he won't listen to me."

"Try, okay? But don't let on that you've been talking to me. That's only going to make things worse."

"You don't think I know that?"

A beat of silence falls between them, then Brett says, "Go talk to my grandmother tomorrow." She gives Jimmy the address. "I'll call her and tell her you're coming. She's lived in Crestwood most of her life. She knows practically everyone in that damn town. If she doesn't recognize the sketch, she can point you in the direction of someone who does."

"I'm going to find him," Jimmy says. "I've got a feeling. Someone here knows something. I just have to knock on the right doors."

She's quiet again, and he wishes he could see the expression on her face, though even then, he isn't sure he'd know what she was thinking. Her silence over the phone is empty and unreadable, so the words he says next are more for him than anything, for the fear knotting his own stomach.

"Don't worry," he says. "Everything's going to work out fine. I'll be back in a few days."

"You'd better be, or I'm coming up there to get you."

"Don't make promises you don't plan on keeping, Bretty," he says, his tone teasing, trying to lighten the mood.

"Don't do anything stupid, Jimmy," she teases him back. "Call me if you find something, okay?"

After they say goodnight, Jimmy slips out of his shoes and changes into a T-shirt to sleep in. It's not even nine o'clock, but after the long drive and tussling with Rausch earlier that day, he's exhausted. He climbs into bed and turns off the light, holding on to the sound of Brett's voice, wrapping it close as he drifts into a restless sleep.

Chapter 14

When Brett told Jimmy about the summers she spent as a girl in Crestwood, he imagined a ramshackle cluster of sea shanties huddled on the edge of wind-shorn cliffs. He imagined narrow alleyways, dead-ends, stone walls slick with brine and rimed in salt. He imagined haunted, hungry eyes peering out at him from behind burlap curtains, townsfolk raised on cold wind and fish bones, rumors and suspicions. When Brett talked about Crestwood, it was always with a certain amount of claustrophobia in her voice, and Jimmy thought he'd be able to drive from one end to the other in the time it took to blink. Now that he's here, driving through the major highway that bisects the town, he can see how wrong he's been in his assumptions.

Crestwood, Washington sprawls along the coastline, tracing the horseshoe shape of Sculpin Bay. There are wind-shorn cliffs, but there are also sandy beaches and green parks and sprawling forests of cedars and pines. There are large industrial areas, too, and several docks, shopping centers, and neighborhoods clustered throughout. A person could live at the base of the Cascade mountain range surrounded by forests or near the Pacific Ocean with sweeping views that extend forever. The town's heart is clearly the historic downtown area, a cluster of red brick buildings nestled steps from Sculpin Bay.

Through gaps between buildings, the ocean shimmers. The breeze smells faintly of salt and fried dough. The streets are old cobblestone and clean. Brightly colored flowers spill from baskets hanging on every lamppost. Flags flap in the wind, advertising an Arts Festival and Fireworks Show happening this weekend. Booths are being set up on the sidewalks. One of the side streets that leads to a beachfront park is blocked off. People wander in and out of small shops, holding bags and coffee cups and the hands of excited children. But they all seem friendly enough, smiling at Jimmy and tipping their heads in greeting as they pass him on the sidewalk. Some even stop and ask if they can pet Trixie, who is all wiggle and excitement from being in a new place with new smells and new people who fawn over her charming brown eyes and soft, floppy ears.

The only haunted, hungry creatures in this town appear to be the seagulls who lurk on eaves and signposts, waiting for someone to drop a muffin.

Jimmy studies the face of every man he walks past. He doesn't actually think it's going to be as easy as that. He still looks because, even though he doesn't think the man he's hunting is here in Crestwood today, if he ever was, perhaps there is some remnant of him left behind. His lingering shadow in the tilt of a chin or the sharp point of a nose or the callous stare of glacial blue eyes.

Jimmy isn't desperate enough yet to stop strangers on the street, show them the sketch, and ask if they recognize the man. But the day is young, and depending on how things go, he and Trixie might very well be back on Main Street later this afternoon, grabbing elbows and making a nuisance of themselves. Before that happens, though, he puts Trixie back in the car that's parked in the public lot beside the library, cracks the windows so she can sniff the cool breeze, and heads to the police station across the street, a gray cement building that looks about as inviting as a shoebox.

A bored-looking man sits behind a glass-enclosed booth in the front lobby. No one else is waiting, so Jimmy goes straight up to the counter and asks to see Stan Harcourt. The man blinks slowly at Jimmy, yawns, stretches his arms over his head, then picks up his desk phone and punches a few numbers.

"There's a man here to see you," he speaks into the receiver, then lifts his eyes back to Jimmy and asks, "What did you say your name was?"

"It's Jimmy Eagan," he answers. "I'm a reporter. Tell him I have some questions about an old case of his. A young woman was murdered in this area about seventeen years ago. Margot Buchanan."

Margot's name doesn't seem to ring a bell with the man. He nods and delivers the information to the person on the other end of the phone, then hangs up. "He'll be right out."

Jimmy sits in one of the lobby's three chairs to wait. A few minutes later, the interior door opens, and a tall, skinny, white man with thinning brown hair steps out. His gaze sweeps over Jimmy, disdain and impatience written all over his face.

"Who the hell are you?" His lip curls in a sneer.

Jimmy stands and offers his hand. "Jimmy Eagan. I'm a reporter with the *Statesman Journal* down in Salem. I'm working on a story about a serial murderer, and I'm following up on a possible lead. I had some questions for you about the Margot Buchanan case? From 1964? I believe you were the lead investigator."

Stan stares at Jimmy's hand for a few seconds. Finally, he sniffs and shakes his head. He fumbles his fingers in his jacket pocket, takes out a pack of cigarettes, and shakes it at Jimmy. "You smoke?"

"No."

"Well, I do." He sticks a cigarette in his mouth and gestures to Jimmy to follow him out the front door into the parking lot.

They walk to a patch of trampled grass between the building

and the road. Cigarette butts litter the ground. Stan lights the cigarette dangling from his lips and, in between puffs, says, "I got a call about you this morning."

Jimmy keeps quiet, staring across the street where a sliver of the bay is visible on the other side of a large parking lot. Three black, long-necked birds bob in the gentle rise and fall of waves near the shoreline. He should have guessed Rausch would make trouble for him, but some part of him hoped that he would have been able to get a few questions in before Rausch made a mess of things.

"That's right," Stan says with an unimpressed laugh. "A detective down in Salem calls me up a few minutes after I clock in this morning and starts yelling at me about a dead girl I'd all but forgotten. Wants to know why I'm handing out confidential information on open cases. I told him I didn't know what the hell he was talking about. Then he said that if you showed up here, I should keep my damn mouth shut and send you packing. He also told me that if you showed up here and girls start coming up missing, I should arrest you immediately and then call him."

Stan twists his eyebrows together as he gives Jimmy a long stare. "Well? What am I supposed to do with that? Should I take you in right now? Lock you up before you start making trouble?"

"Could you just look at this sketch for me?" Jimmy takes the paper from his pocket, deciding then and there that everything else can wait.

The questions he has about the investigation, or lack of one, the questions about Stan's only suspect, the gut feelings and instincts, things that never made it into any of the reports—those questions can all come later. After he gets a lead on this man. If he ever gets a lead. Maybe he won't. Maybe this is a dead-end like every other dead-end he's run up against in the past two years since Cherish Spalding's murder. Maybe whoever is killing these girls, whoever killed Margot, is a phantom, a shapeshifter, slipping through time and space, immaterial.

Jimmy holds the sketch in the air between them. Stan reaches for it, but Jimmy doesn't trust him and pulls it from his nicotine-stained fingers. The cop rolls his eyes, but curiosity gets the best of him. He squints at the image, but only for a second, his gaze darting away so fast Jimmy can't be sure he even really looked at it.

"There's no one around here who looks like that," Stan says, taking one last puff on his cigarette before dropping the butt to the ground with the others.

"What about in 1964?" Jimmy carefully folds the sketch and tucks it back into his pocket.

Stan snorts a laugh. "I can't even remember what I ate for breakfast this morning. You think I'm going to remember everyone who was hanging around this town seventeen years ago?"

"So you didn't bring anyone in as a suspect who looked like him?" A flicker of hope at the base of Jimmy's throat that this will be easy and the kid Stan liked as a suspect in 1964 will be the same man in the sketch, but Stan's frown tells him he's not going to get so lucky today.

"I told you I've never seen anyone around here who looks like that."

Jimmy decides to push Stan a little, get him riled up to see what slips out. "You must have had some thoughts on who killed Margot Buchanan, though. Case like that, you don't really expect me to believe you forgot about it. A young woman, a pretty girl, the granddaughter of a prominent family is brutally murdered, the killer's never found, and the cop who investigated it moves on like it was nothing? That sounds awfully convenient to me."

"Are you accusing me of something?" His cheeks flush red.

"I'm just wondering if you might have a reason for pretending you don't recognize this man." Jimmy shakes the paper a little.

Stan sputters. His hands fumble again in his pockets, but he seems to decide against another cigarette because he lets his hands drop to his side. "I'm not pretending, you little shit. I said I've never seen him because I've never seen him."

Jimmy shrugs. "If you say so."

"You're a real piece of work, you know that." With each word, his voice gets louder. "You're a blood-sucking leech trying to get rich off other people's miseries while the rest of us are just trying to do our goddamn jobs. So here's what you're going to do." He jabs his finger into Jimmy's chest. "You're going to climb back inside whatever beat-up piece of shit you call a car and get the hell out of my town. If I see you so much as stopping for gas, I'm dragging your ass to jail and throwing away the key. Are we clear?"

A car door slams, and from across the parking lot, a man shouts, "Everything okay over there, Stan?"

Stan and Jimmy both look over to where a uniformed officer stands with his feet spread wide, and his arms crossed over his chest. He's about Jimmy's age, with dirty-blond hair buzzed short in typical cop fashion. He squints against the brightness of the sun, lifting his hand to block the light as he inspects Jimmy from a distance.

Stan waves his hand dismissively. "It's fine, Eli. Just giving this man directions to the freeway."

Eli watches them for a few more seconds, like he's waiting for Stan to change his mind and call him over, or waiting for Jimmy to do something stupid. When neither thing happens, he crosses the parking lot and disappears into the precinct.

Stan leans close to Jimmy, the heat of his breath reeking of smoke. "This town has suffered enough over that girl's death. We don't need you here digging up old hurts. Whatever monsters you're dealing with in Salem have nothing to do with us."

He gives Jimmy one last menacing glare then walks away, leaving him standing there beside a pile of spent cigarette butts. Jimmy nudges the trash with the toe of his shoe. He didn't come here looking for trouble; he came to get out of the trouble he's already in. Stan can bellow and threaten all he wants, but Jimmy came to Crestwood for answers, and he's not leaving until he finds them.

CHAPTER 15

The house on Bayshore Drive is easy to find. It's the only house painted yellow with a fairytale castle turret jutting off one corner. The other houses on Bayshore Drive are newer construction, modern lines, functional architecture. Brett's grandparents' house, on the other hand, is whimsy and delight. It stands like a lighthouse on a small spit of land. A neatly trimmed lawn slopes down to a pebbled beach and a private dock with a small boathouse painted the same yellow as the house.

The woman who answers the front door has Brett's cheekbones and the same cynical glint in her eyes like she's been disappointed by the world one too many times. After Jimmy introduces himself and Trixie, the hard outer shell falls away, and Anita Wilson turns soft and welcoming.

"Yes, Brett told me you might be stopping by. I've made some coffee. There's enough for you if you'd like some." She laughs, a broken-hearted sound, and says, "I always make enough for me and Frank. Frank was my husband. He's been gone going on two years now, but my hand still puts in that extra scoop every time. Habit, I guess. Hard to break a lifetime of making coffee for two people."

She smiles at Jimmy, and Jimmy smiles back. Brett told him

a few months ago about her grandfather's recent death, a heart attack, and how Anita was struggling to adjust to a life alone after some sixty years of marriage.

"I'm sorry for your loss, Mrs. Wilson," he says, as he steps inside and follows her through the house to the kitchen.

"Oh, we get by. And please, call me Anita." She tells him it's okay to let Trixie off her leash. "She's housebroken, right?"

"Yes," Jimmy says. "Since she was a puppy. Well, she's still a puppy, actually. She's only about ten months old."

Trixie's nose is pinned to the floor as she sniffs a winding trail that eventually leads her to the refrigerator. Anita reaches for the door, laughing. "She's a smart girl, isn't she? Is it okay if I give her hot dogs?"

Jimmy nods. Anita takes a pack from the fridge and carries it with her to the table. Periodically during their conversation, she drops pieces of the processed meat to Trixie who's sitting politely at her feet.

"So, you're here because of Margot?" Anita takes a break from Trixie to pour Jimmy a steaming cup of coffee.

Jimmy nods and stirs sugar into his cup. The table in the corner has a perfect view of the small boathouse and dock. Gray water laps the shore. A half-moon string of islands curves against the horizon, blue and hazy behind a thin mist. Trixie sits at Anita's feet, gazing up at her, begging for more snacks. Anita obliges.

"I'll tell you whatever you want to know," she says to Jimmy. "Whatever I can remember, that is. Though I have to warn you, my mind isn't as sharp as it used to be." With a sad smile, she taps one finger against her temple. "But if you think it might help, I'll answer any questions you have. Brett said you read the report from the initial investigation? That there really wasn't much there?"

"Yeah, it was pretty sparse."

"We didn't have much to tell them." She goes on to explain

what Jimmy already knows, the things he read in the file. How Margot went missing on Tuesday morning. "Brett was the last person to see her. They were hanging out on the dock, swimming and splashing around, and then Margot took off. Brett couldn't tell us where Margot went. Of course, she didn't come to us right away. It was only after Margot didn't come home for dinner, when I asked Brett if she'd seen her sister, only then that she told us she hadn't seen Margot since before noon." Her hands curl tighter around the coffee cup as she shakes her head. "I don't blame her. Of course not. Things were so different back then. The girls were always off by themselves. This town. It was safe. We thought it was safe. It's the kind of place where we look out for one another. Things like this. What happened to Margot. Things like that aren't supposed to happen here."

She takes a breath, her eyes darting toward the french doors, staring out through the glass toward the ocean. Absently, her hand strokes the top of Trixie's head.

"It wasn't Brett's fault," she says quietly. "Though that poor girl has spent most of her life since then blaming herself. We couldn't have known. Margot would go off with her older friends a lot. She did her best to include Brett, but you know how it goes. Do you have siblings, Jimmy?"

"No, ma'am."

"Well, Margot loved Brett, and she did her best to make sure she didn't feel left out, but there was still an age difference between them. Margot was seventeen. She was more independent, more grown-up. And Brett was only thirteen, still so much a little girl. Understandably, Margot needed a break from her little sister from time to time. She would sometimes leave Brett at the house and go off with her friends and not return until after dark. It wasn't the first time she had missed dinner, but it was the first time I worried about her." Anita's hand darts to her face, swiping at tears gathering on her lashes. "I don't know why. There was something in the air that day, an electric heat, something unsettled in my soul. I tried to ignore it. 'You're being ridiculous, Anita,' I told myself. That girl's just fine. She wasn't, though, was she?"

A faint smile plays on her lips, a smile twisted up in her grief.

Jimmy lays the sketch on the table in front of her. The wrinkles in Anita's forehead deepen as she bends for a closer look. Her fingers brush the edge of the paper as if she's afraid to touch it. "Is this him?"

Under the table, Trixie lets out the quietest of whines and lays her head across Anita's feet.

"This is someone who might be a person of interest, yes," Jimmy says. "I'd like to find him. I'd like to talk to him. Is he familiar to you?"

Anita studies the sketch more intensely, taking her time, tilting her head one way and then the other. He can see in her face that she wants to know this man, that she's trying to recognize the slope of his nose and the tight grimace of his lips, the right eye that sits slightly higher on his face than the left. In the end, she shakes her head.

She pushes the paper across the table to Jimmy. "I'm sorry. I don't know him."

She drops another bite of hot dog under the table for Trixie, who snatches it off the floor like she's never eaten a day in her life.

"This is a recent sketch," Jimmy says. "The woman encountered this man about a year ago. If he was here in Crestwood the summer Margot died, he might look quite a bit different than this. Younger, maybe with a beard or shorter hair? Maybe he was one of the friends she hung out with? Maybe he was heavier back then, or maybe the shape of his face was different?"

Anita thinks a minute, then shakes her head again, a frown tugging on the corners of her mouth. "I'm sorry. I wish I knew him.

I wish I could tell you exactly who he is, but no, I'm sorry. I don't recognize him at all. The boys Margot hung out with that summer, they're all still here. Oh sure, a few went away to college, but they came back. This town draws people back."

She drinks the last of her coffee, then gets up and takes the mug to the sink. Trixie, tail wagging, follows at her heels. "Have you spoken with Danny Cyrus yet? He's the boy the detective was really interested in right after it happened. The whole town thought he did it, of course. Some still do."

"I'd like to talk to him, yes," Jimmy says. "Do you know where I can find him?"

"Oh, sure." Anita scratches directions onto a piece of paper. "He's living out on his brother-in-law's property near Lake Chastain. Now, be careful with that one. He came back from Vietnam a changed man. He used to work for Frank at the packing plant before it shut down, so I know he's not a bad person. He's just rough around the edges. Mostly bark. I just wouldn't put my hand next to his food dish if you catch my meaning."

She gives Jimmy a warning look, then her face spreads into a warm smile, and she lowers herself to the floor, taking Trixie's head in both hands and giving her a mighty scratch. "You and Trixie are welcome over here anytime, Jimmy. Any friend of Brett's is a friend of mine, and what you're doing for our family, it's kind of you. It truly is."

She returns to the table where Jimmy is sitting and pats his cheek. Her hand is warm and soft.

"I hope you find him." Her eyes shift to the sketch still lying on the table. "It would be good to be able to put all of this behind us once and for all."

Chapter 16

Jimmy drives to Lake Chastain with the windows down. Trixie shoves her head into the wind, lapping the air with her tongue, her ears billowing like sails. Her grin is wide and sloppy, drool streams from her lips. Dappled light scatters through the canopy of pine trees and alders heavy with spring leaves, turning the air a saturated green. A fine dusting of pollen stains the tarmac yellow.

As Jimmy approaches the turn-off Anita described—the tilted blue mailbox, the No Trespassing sign, the barbed-wire fence—a brown rabbit steps from the underbrush onto the shoulder. The animal tenses and twitches its ears. Trixie, catching the scent, tips her head back and howls. The rabbit darts back into the bushes.

Before Jimmy can turn into the driveway, a pickup truck emerges from the shadows, and Jimmy has no choice but to drive past it. He slows enough to glimpse the driver of the pickup, a heavyset man with light brown hair long enough it's starting to curl around his ears. He fits the description Anita gave of Danny Cyrus.

Jimmy turns into the next pullout and glances in his rearview mirror. The pickup truck rattles past him and keeps going. Jimmy pulls his car onto the highway behind the pickup and, keeping his distance, follows it to a park at the edge of Lake Chastain.

It's nearing noon on a Saturday, the start of a holiday weekend, and the parking lot is filling up quickly. Trucks drop off their ski and fishing boats at the ramp. Motors spew unburned fuel into the air as the boats rumble away from the dock, sending small waves splashing to shore. Kids scream and chase one another on the long pebbled beach near the boat ramp. Mothers carry picnic baskets and sunscreen into the shade. Fathers drag coolers and bags of charcoal briquettes to the grills dotting the shoreline.

Not wanting to draw attention to himself, Jimmy parks on the other side of the lot from the spot Danny chooses. Though the place is so busy, he doubts the other man even noticed a car following him here.

Danny gets out of his pickup, grabs a fishing pole and other gear from the cargo bed, and walks toward the lake. He walks past the dock and boat ramp and the families setting up their picnics. After a few minutes following the curve of the lake north, he disappears from sight.

When Jimmy opens the passenger door, Trixie leaps from the car, darts toward a clump of bushes, and begins sniffing in circles. He whistles for her, and she hurries to his side. Once she gets a sense of where they're headed, though, she takes off ahead of him, her nose pressed to the ground, snorting and snuffling, chasing down the faded scents of whatever creatures were here before her.

Jimmy finds Danny Cyrus about a quarter-mile from the parking lot, standing on a peninsula of uneven rocks that juts into the lake. Trixie runs up to him first, her tongue slopping from the side of her mouth as she wags her whole body, bumping against Danny's legs hard enough he loses his balance. Regaining his footing, he bends to pet Trixie. He looks up at the sound of Jimmy crunching through the underbrush.

"This your dog?"

"Sure is," Jimmy says, adopting a laid-back but slightly apologetic tone. "Sorry about that. Come here, girl. Trixie, come."

She returns to Jimmy's side, then catches the scent of something in the trees and wanders off.

"I always did like beagles," Danny says and dips his hand into a white cup. "Loyal dogs, so long as they don't smell a rabbit."

He spears a wriggling worm on the end of a hook.

"What kind of fish do you catch out here?" Jimmy squints across the water where the mid-afternoon sun glints like diamonds off the lake's smooth surface.

"Trout, mostly. Some smallmouth bass. Perch."

A fish leaps from the water about twenty feet from where Danny's standing. It's a flash of silver that makes the smallest of splashes before disappearing. Ripples roll across the water's surface.

Danny turns away from Jimmy and flicks his rod. The reel makes a whirring sound as the line's cast. The baited hook drops into the water a few inches from where the fish jumped. Danny keeps his eyes fixed on the red and white bobber floating on the surface, his body language warning off any further conversation.

Jimmy ignores it and steps onto the peninsula. "You're Danny Cyrus, aren't you?"

A muscle in the other man's jaw tenses. With one hand keeping hold of the fishing rod, he dips the other down, takes a beer from a small cooler on the ground beside him, and cracks it open with one hand.

"I guess that depends on who's asking." Danny takes a long drink, then wipes the back of his hand across his mouth and belches.

"I heard that if I'm looking for someone, you're the guy I should talk to."

Danny swings his head around. "Who told you that?"

Jimmy shrugs. "Just people."

"In my experience, people don't know what the hell they're talking about most of the time." Danny takes another drink and tugs on the fishing rod, repositioning the hook, bait, and bobber.

The bushes along the shoreline rustle as Trixie emerges from the trees, apparently losing or growing bored with whatever scent she was tracking. There are a few pine needles in her fur and mud splatters on her white socks. She joins Jimmy and Danny on the peninsula, finds a flat rock in the sun, and lies down with a dramatic sigh.

"So, you wouldn't know where I could find this man?" Jimmy steps close enough to Danny to show him the sketch.

Danny glances at the paper, then squints out over the lake. "What's he done?"

"Nothing."

Danny snorts in disbelief. "He owe you money or something?"

"Sure, let's say he does."

"I don't know him." But when he says it, his shoulders stiffen. He stares into the distance and tugs on the fishing line as if it's the most interesting thing in the world. If Jimmy were a betting man, he'd put all his money on Danny being a liar.

"You know what else people told me?" Jimmy tucks the picture away in his pocket. "They told me I should stay away from you. That you're dangerous."

"Like I said...people don't know what the hell they're talking about most of the time."

"So when they told me you killed a girl out here seventeen years ago, I shouldn't believe that either?" Jimmy gestures to the pines edging the lake. They spread for miles in every direction.

Jimmy remembers reading in Margot Buchanan's police file that there are hiking trails throughout this whole area. Somewhere near here, her body was discovered.

Danny tenses. The beer can in his hand crumples as he squeezes it in his fist. He tosses the empty can to the ground and whirls to face Jimmy. Sensing the sudden change in emotions, Trixie rises to her feet and presses herself against Jimmy's leg.

"Who the hell are you? And what do you want from me?" Danny grips the fishing rod like he might use it to smack Jimmy across the face.

Trixie whines. Jimmy takes a small step back.

Danny's a big man, bigger than Jimmy by a good half a foot and one hundred pounds easy. Jimmy's not a fighter, either. He's never hit anything or anyone in his life. If he went fist to fist with Danny, he'd lose. He holds his hands up in the air, trying to deescalate the situation.

"If it helps, I don't believe them," Jimmy says. "I don't think you had anything to do with Margot's death."

Danny flinches at the sound of her name and turns back to the water, his attention on fishing again. He reels in the line a little bit, then lets it out. The wind tugs it across the surface of the lake away from shore.

"That man in the picture," he says quietly, his voice unsteady. "You think he might be the one who did it?"

"I'm looking into the possibility, yes."

Danny props the end of his fishing rod between two small rocks, then turns to Jimmy and holds out his hand. "Let me see it again."

Jimmy passes him the sketch. Danny studies it a moment before giving it back.

"She was hanging out with a lot of guys that summer, not just me. He might have been one of 'em." Danny bends to pick up his rod again, reeling the line in. He plucks the worm he was using as bait off the hook and tosses it into the water. "I don't know. It was a long time ago. His face looks familiar, but I don't know his name or where he lives now. It's not here. Wherever he went, I know for sure he's not in Crestwood anymore."

Danny gathers his gear.

"You know for sure?" Jimmy presses him.

With the rod tucked under one arm, tackle box under the other, cooler strap dangling from his left hand, Danny says, "I'm not a nice man. I don't hang out with nice people. Get told long enough that you're a villain, and you eventually become one. I know every degenerate, dick, and Harry in this godforsaken town, and he's not one of them." He tips his head toward the picture still clutched in Jimmy's hand. "I suppose he could be upper crust or keeping his head down among the nine-to-five dads and PTA moms, but something tells me probably not. Plus, I know them, too. Everyone has a little darkness in them, don't they?"

He flashes Jimmy a grin, and Jimmy gets the feeling he dodged a bullet today, that he could have ended up with a black eye, or worse, ended up in the lake as fish food.

"Thanks for your help," Jimmy says to Danny's retreating back.

Over his shoulder, Danny calls, "If you find him, tell him to come see me. Seems like the two of us have some unfinished business."

Jimmy and Trixie spend over an hour thrashing through the woods around Lake Chastain. Some part of him hopes to find a memorial, a bench with Margot's name on it, a plaque hammered into a nearby tree, something to commemorate her violent death. But there's nothing. He doesn't know if he's in the right spot. He doesn't even know what he's looking for, really. It's been almost seventeen years. Of course there's nothing here. Tired, hungry, frustrated, Jimmy scratches at one of a hundred mosquito bites on the back of his arm and whistles for Trixie. She comes bounding out of the brush with the kind of energy that tells him she could keep doing this for as long as he let her.

They retrace their steps back to the parking lot. Twenty minutes later, he's parked in the public lot beside the library again, under the shade of a spreading elm tree. He gives Trixie some water and treats before leaving her to go get his own food in the café across the street.

Crumbles and Cakes is crowded even though it's the middle of the afternoon. Jimmy orders a sandwich and coffee at the counter and manages to find a table in the corner after a retired couple leave. He takes out his notebook and scratches a few notes.

Other boyfriends?

Transient?

What am I not seeing?

Jimmy spreads the sketch of his suspect out on the table. He takes a picture of Margot from his pocket and lays it next to the sketch. Brett gave the photograph to him a few weeks ago, shortly after she told him about Margot's murder. He asked for it, for a picture of Margot alive and smiling, so that he could remember her as more than a corpse rotting in the weeds. He wants to remember why he's doing this and who he's doing this for. Margot was a pretty girl with golden-blond hair and an infectious smile. In this picture, she's sitting on a tire swing with Brett. The sisters have their arms around one another. Brett leans her head on Margot's shoulder. Her lips are stained red from the half-melted, cherry popsicle she's holding in her other hand.

Someone bumps Jimmy's chair. He jostles, and his pen drops to the floor. He reaches to grab it at the same time as the woman who bumped into him does. Their hands brush, and her eyes flicker to his. They're a bright blue but hard as flint. Her lips tighten over her teeth, and she looks like she's about to say something cruel to him.

A young girl's voice interrupts, "Mom? Hurry up. We're going to be late."

The woman lets go of the pen and straightens. She smooths her hands down her skirt, and her gaze flicks to the sketch and photograph lying together on the table. It's subtle, the way her fingers curl against her leg, the slight flare of her nostrils, how she jerks her head back like she's been slapped. She recognizes him, Jimmy realizes. The man in the sketch is someone she knows.

"Mom?" A girl around ten or eleven and wearing a soccer jersey comes up behind the woman and touches her elbow. Her brown hair is pulled into a high ponytail.

The woman's expression shifts again, turning neutral and unbothered. Whatever she was thinking a few seconds ago, it's gone now, sunk beneath the surface of her pale, smooth skin and vacant, blue eyes.

"Yes, Elizabeth, I heard you the first time." She grabs her daughter's hand and drags her from the café.

Jimmy is about to go after her when another woman appears beside the table with his sandwich and cup of coffee. She's older, her auburn hair dusted white. He can't tell if it's flour in her hair or if she's going gray. When she smiles at him, wrinkles crease her face in a pleasing way. Tied around her waist is an apron printed with the name of the café.

"Just moved in or just visiting?" she asks, her voice a warm hug. She sets his order on the corner of the table and, seeing the sketch, lets out a hum of surprise. With her fingertips, she moves the paper to see it better. "Funny, that looks like my sister's boy."

Jimmy's whole body goes tense. "You know him?"

The woman lifts her hand off the sketch and takes a small step back. "I'm sure it's a coincidence. There are plenty of men around here and all over the place who look like that."

But she can't take her eyes off the picture, her gaze tracing down the slender line of his nose, the mouth that's pinched in a grimace, his uneven eyes. "It's a pretty good likeness, though, isn't it. Of course, my eyesight isn't what it used to be, and I haven't seen him in so long…but I suppose it could be Archer. I'm sorry. Why do you have that picture? Are you an artist or…?"

"I'm a reporter," he says. "I'm looking for him. For this man. Archer, you said? He's your nephew?"

"Well, Archer's my nephew, yes, but I don't know if that picture you have is of him or not." She points at the sketch. "Why are you looking for him? Has he done something wrong?"

"When was the last time you saw your nephew?"

She thinks for a minute, then says, "Oh, it's been a long time. He stayed with us one summer. Now, when was that? Nearly seventeen years ago. Hard to believe, but yes, it was the summer of 1964. The same summer that Anita Wilson's granddaughter was killed."

A chill runs through Jimmy. Cold, then hot, then cold again. The woman frowns and shakes her head as if she's remembering something she'd rather not, as if she can feel it, too—the secrets of the past rising to the surface. Someone calls to her from behind the counter. She wipes her hands on her apron and flashes Jimmy a polite smile.

"I'm sorry. I can't really talk about this right now. One of my cooks called in sick today, and we're running behind in the kitchen. But if you want, please come back this evening. We close up at six. My son will be here by then, too, and he can have a look at that picture of yours. He'll know for sure if that's Archer or not. He's got a better memory than me." Her smile brightens at the mention of her son. Then she gestures to the sandwich, which is a grilled pastrami and Swiss on rye, and says, "Better eat up before it gets soggy."

CHAPTER 17

Jimmy checks out of the motel room a day earlier than planned. The entire drive back to Salem, the name Mary Andress gave him turns to an incantation.

Archer French.

Archer French.

It beats a rhythm in his head that matches the pulse of headlights going the opposite direction on the freeway.

Archer French.

It becomes a spell, a wish. Say it enough times and the monster will be made flesh, and Jimmy might finally have his answers.

When Jimmy returned to the café earlier this evening, the final customers were on their way out the door. A young man with thinning hair and a scraggly beard moved between the tables with a dishrag, swiping crumbs onto the floor, re-centering the small vases with plastic flowers. He glanced up when Jimmy walked in and said, "We're closed."

Before Jimmy could explain himself, the woman he spoke with before swept from the back of the café. "It's all right, Nathan," she said. "He's here to talk to me."

She smiled at Jimmy and held her hand out. "I don't think I

properly introduced myself earlier. Mary Andress. I own this place." There was pride in her voice as she swept her gaze around the café. "Do you want anything to drink? Coffee? Tea? On the house." Mary flapped her hand at the man wiping tables. "Nathan, be a dear and get us a fresh pot of coffee. That's my son," she said to Jimmy.

When Nathan returned with the coffee, Mary pulled a chair out from one of the tables and sat down. "Show him the picture," she said. And when Jimmy gave the sketch to Nathan, she asked, "Who does that look like to you?"

It's almost midnight by the time Jimmy takes the freeway off-ramp into Salem. He spent all of one day in Crestwood. He could have stayed another night, he'd already paid for the motel room, but he didn't want to waste any more time. The hotel manager seemed more than happy to have him check out early.

When Jimmy pulls into his apartment complex, Trixie lifts her head from where she's been curled in a ball on the passenger seat and yawns. The entire two minutes it takes to walk upstairs to his apartment, Jimmy worries he's going to find the door hanging open, the place ransacked again. But luck continues to be on his side. The door is locked. The apartment is in the same condition as how he left it yesterday afternoon. He dumps his duffel bag by the door and walks straight to the living room. Trixie's toenails click across the linoleum as she makes her way into the kitchen to check her empty food dish.

There's nothing left on the living room wall but a couple of thumbtacks and ripped pieces of tape. Rausch took everything else as evidence. It's evidence, all right, even if they're trying to use it against the wrong man.

No matter. Jimmy doesn't need it.

He takes the photograph Mary Andress gave him before he left Crestwood and pins it to the center of the wall. He works from memory, scribbling dates, cities, and names onto scraps of paper and tacking those scraps to the wall. Piece by piece, he recreates what was there before. A timeline for the August girls, a way to track the Ophelia Killer and connect him to Archer French, to see if it all fits the way Jimmy hopes it will.

According to what Mary told him, her nephew was a smart boy but was constantly getting in trouble. He'd talk back to his teachers at school and harass girls in the hallways, pushing them down, taking their books and ripping out the pages, trying to see under their skirts. He was a wild boy, an angry boy who lashed out at anyone who got in his way. Even, and sometimes especially, his own mother, a woman who Mary admitted should probably have never been a mother in the first place. She could be cold and distant, cruel, too. But the biggest problem, Mary said, was her inconsistency. She was loving to Archer one minute, ignoring him the next, and didn't have the first clue about what it meant to discipline an unruly child.

What Archer needed, Mary said, was a steady schedule and a good, hard whooping. What Archer needed was structure and discipline and responsible men to look up to, not the strangers his mother was bringing in and out of the house, a new man every week. Wanting to help, Mary secured Archer a job on a fishing boat for the summer after he graduated high school. He was in Crestwood from the end of May to the beginning of September in 1964 when he went back to Eugene to start his freshman year at the University of Oregon.

Jimmy studies the wall. In 1967, a young woman was killed in Medford. The very same year Archer French dropped out of school. Though, forced out might be a better description.

Something happened, Mary told Jimmy, pouring them all another cup of coffee. She wasn't sure of the details, having only heard the story secondhand from her sister. It seemed Archer got into some trouble over a young woman who claimed she'd been attacked outside the library. She fought him off, kicking and spitting and screaming for help. When the police came to talk to Archer, he denied having any involvement. He worked in the library, yes, but claimed he had never seen the girl before in his life. The police apparently believed him because no one was arrested. The young woman never pressed charges, and that was the end of that.

Except, according to Mary, Archer was so shaken by the accusations, he stopped going to classes, stopped going to work, stopped hanging out with friends. In March, he dropped out of school entirely. Five months later, a woman's body was found in Medford with her tongue cut out.

Archer tried to sign up for the Marines, but they wouldn't take him. Mary wasn't sure why. Eventually, he started working as a janitor at a high school in Eugene, but according to Mary, he struggled to make ends meet. He kept getting fired and had to move apartments. Many times over the next two years, he called Mary asking for money. She gave him a little bit each time, but each time encouraged him to move back to Bend, where his mother lived. Mary couldn't say with certainty, but she thought Archer may have lived a few months in Brownsville during the spring and summer of 1968. By 1969, he was back in Eugene. That August, Lydia Rhodes was found murdered, her tongue removed.

Archer's mother was diagnosed with advanced-stage breast cancer in early 1970. There wasn't much the doctors could do to treat it. She was dying. According to Mary, Archer moved to Bend shortly after that to help care for her.

Jimmy paces in front of the wall. Trixie hops onto the couch and lies down. She tracks his motion with her eyes.

August 1970, August 1971, August 1972 are blank spaces on the wall. If girls were killed during those years, Jimmy hasn't found them yet. Then, in 1973, Archers' mother died. Mary lost track of him after that.

"I have no idea where he is now," she said, getting up to collect the coffee cups and carry them into the back of the café. "The last time we saw him was at my sister's funeral in June of '73. He seemed to be doing okay. He had a job, another janitorial position, I think. And he was talking about signing up at the community college, finishing up his degree. He was sad, of course, we all were, but there was some relief, too. She'd been sick for so long, and he was the one who'd been taking care of her. After she died, that was his opportunity to really start over, I think. To really try and make something of himself. A few months later, I tried calling him, but the phone number, the only one I had for him, had been disconnected."

"Did you try and find out where he went?" Jimmy asked.

Mary shook her head. "He's an adult now. He's responsible for himself. He can make his own choices." She frowned at the sketch still lying on the table, a flicker of worry darkened her eyes, then she blinked, and her smile returned, though it was strained this time, thin and brittle. "I've got too much on my plate as it is to keep track of someone who doesn't want to bother having a relationship with me. I can give you the last address I had for him if you think it will help."

Jimmy left Crestwood with a last-known address in Bend and a more recent picture of Archer at his mother's funeral. Mary had unburied the photograph from a stack of old paperwork in the office of her café. Jimmy left with a name and a sinking feeling that all of this could just be sending him straight to another dead-end.

But as Jimmy works over the new details he got from Mary, as he puts the pieces back together and the pattern on the wall emerges, the tightening in his gut becomes one of excitement, not dread. It's the same anticipation he got when he read Lydia Rhodes' autopsy report for the first time. His pulse quickens. He can't sit still. He knows this is the man he's looking for. He knows with a certainty that he doesn't bother second-guessing. Archer French is the Ophelia Killer. Now all he has to do is track the bastard down and hand him over to the cops.

That night, Jimmy falls asleep stretched out on the floor, looking at the wall from upside-down. Trixie curls into a ball beside him, snoring lightly.

The following day, Jimmy wakes with a knot in his back that's hard to work out and a single-minded determination to track down Archer French and make him answer for the things he's done.

A crisp blue fog blanketed the valley overnight. It's not like the fog in winter that smothers the sky for weeks, but a spring fog that will burn off by noon, exposing brilliant skies and a butter-yellow sun. Jimmy takes Trixie on a long walk, using the gray obscurity to his advantage. With the details of the world around him smudged, he finds it easier to focus on Archer French. By the time he gets home, he knows exactly what to do next.

He starts in the most obvious place—the phone book. There are no Archer French's listed in the Salem area, but he spends all of Sunday calling the sixteen other Frenchs listed. None of them know the man he's looking for.

His next step is to contact the administrators at the University of Oregon. But here, his search grinds to a halt. Everything's closed for the holiday weekend. So he spends Monday pacing his living room and going back over his notes in case he's missed something.

First thing Tuesday morning, he calls the university. After confirming Archer French was indeed an undergrad student between 1964 and 1967 but never finished his degree, Jimmy moves on to his contacts in Bend. One high school vice principal, one pastor, and one funeral home director later, and Jimmy confirms French lived with his mother in Bend until she died in 1972. After that, he becomes harder to track, but Jimmy manages to find a forwarding address to an apartment complex in Gresham.

He calls the manager, who says he's never heard of Archer

French, but he only just took over the place. All the records are a mess, and Jimmy thinks this will be where it ends until the manager says, wait, no, here's something. Archer French. Yes, he lived here for a year and left a forwarding address to an apartment in Corvallis. One August girl. And then he moved on. From there, it gets easier. The closer Jimmy gets, the stronger the scent. In every place Archer French has lived, a girl has died, her body left in the woods, flowers clutched to her bosom, her tongue taken.

On Wednesday morning, with adrenaline and too many cups of coffee churning through his blood, Jimmy grabs his car keys and drives south to Corvallis. He doesn't have an appointment, but the university soccer coach agrees to see him anyway. She's a harsh-looking woman with a perpetual scowl. As she pulls the photograph of Archer French close to her face, her cheeks flush red.

"This is him." She rattles the photograph in the air. "This is the creep I caught in the locker room. I'm sure of it."

Jimmy takes the photograph to the security office, then the dean's office. After being sent in circles, Jimmy finally talks with a woman in human resources who recognizes Archer French's photograph.

"Yes," she says, digging through the paperwork for contact information. "He worked for us as a janitor for a few months in 1975. We had to fire him."

"What for?"

"We were getting complaints from some of the girls' dormitories. He was...lingering. They weren't comfortable with him cleaning their common areas. When I brought him in to discuss it, he became belligerent, called me some names I won't repeat. I decided then it was easier to fire him. Yes, here it is. This is the address he gave us to send his last paycheck."

She writes it down on a piece of paper and hands the paper to Jimmy.

He thanks her and takes the paper. The address is in Salem,

but it's at least six years old. Since then, Archer French could have moved several times, but this is the closest Jimmy's been so far. He'll go tomorrow, he decides, take Trixie for company, drive past the address, and see what he can find.

He tells no one his plans. Not Tadd. Not Brett. There's nothing to tell. Not really. He's got nothing but a six-year-old address and a gut feeling. Even if he had more to go on, Jimmy still isn't sure he'd tell them anything yet. He doesn't want anyone talking him out of what he decided to do long before he ever heard the name Archer French. Neither does he want to write this story with whatever watered-down version of the truth the police will send out in a press release after it's all over.

For years, Jimmy's been the only one hunting a monster. He's not going to quit now, not when he's so damn close.

Chapter 18

On Thursday morning, Jimmy parks on the street in front of a gray and white ranch house at the end of a suburban cul-de-sac. The lawn is brown. Weeds grow from cracks in the asphalt. The house looks tired but not entirely dilapidated. A dark blue sedan sits in the driveway, but the curtains are drawn over the windows. No way to tell if anyone's home except by going up and knocking on the door.

Jimmy gets out of the car. Trixie follows. She sticks close to his side as he walks up the short driveway and circles the sedan, snapping pictures of the license plate and a crust of mud under the front bumper. He peers through the car windows. There are some crumpled fast-food wrappers in the passenger footwell and a small pile of cigarette butts in the ashtray. Otherwise, the inside looks clean. It could be the car the girls described lurking outside their house at night, or it could belong to any number of other people who don't stalk and murder young women.

"Ready, Trix?" Jimmy mutters under his breath as he bends to tie a rope around her neck. He keeps it loose and gives her a piece of hot dog as a treat. She bumps her nose against his hand, wanting more. He promises she can have the whole package as soon as this is over, then straightens and walks her up to the front door.

Before he can knock, the door swings open. A man wearing a white tank top and gray sweatpants glares out at them.

"What the hell are you doing creeping around my house?" His voice is gruff.

"Is this your dog?" Jimmy gestures to Trixie. "She was running loose, and I'm checking with all the neighbors to see if anyone recognizes her."

The man opens the door wider to get a better look at Trixie, who stares up at him expectantly. Her tail whips the air.

The angles of the man's face are sharper in person, but Jimmy is certain this is Archer French. The man in the sketch. The man who spent a summer in Crestwood. The monster, who for seventeen years, hid in plain sight.

"She doesn't have a collar," Jimmy says.

Archer crouches in front of Trixie and holds out his hand. Trixie sniffs his fingers, then flattens her ears and backs away. Archer shakes his head. "I've never seen her before. Good looking dog, though."

He stands up again and moves to shut the door. Jimmy realizes the flaw in his plan. Though he's come up with a way to get Archer to open the door, he now needs an excuse to get inside.

"Could I use your phone?" The words fall out in a rush. "I can't really take care of her. My apartment doesn't allow dogs. And I'm a little allergic. Could I use your phone to call animal control?"

Tension spreads across Archer's shoulders. His ice-blue eyes narrow to thin slits. Jimmy almost walks it back, almost says, it's all right, never mind. There's still time for him and Trixie to tuck tail and go home, call the police and tell them to come and do their damn jobs. Except then, he wouldn't get the story. He would be at Rausch's whim when it came to details, and the details are everything.

You'd be famous, Slim Jim, Rausch had taunted him. *Isn't that why you do this? Why you go to so much trouble? You can't say no to that front-page story.*

Jimmy always believed his work to be more honest than that, more respectable. He tells the truth. He fits the pieces together until it makes sense. He exposes the dark underbelly of society in an effort to keep the rest of them safe. That's what he thought he did. But now, standing here on Archer French's front porch, lying about Trixie, pretending to be someone he's not, he's not so sure anymore. Maybe he's exactly the kind of man Rausch described. A man willing to risk everything for the most important byline of his career. He already knows what the headline will be:

INSIDE THE MONSTER'S LAIR

"It'll only take a minute." He smiles at Archer.

Archer's tongue moves over the sharp point of his incisor, his lips curling into a sneer, but he steps back and opens the door wider, inviting Jimmy and Trixie inside. "Let me find you a phone book."

Trixie doesn't want to go in. She digs in stubbornly and pulls back on the rope, trying to wriggle free of it. For a second, Jimmy senses her fear through the tension of the rope. For a second, he hears Brett's voice, an echo of warning, *Don't do anything stupid.* He'll be careful. In and out. A few minutes, that's all it will take. He just wants a quick look around. He wants to find something concrete, something he can bring to Rausch. These are the lies he tells himself as he steps into Archer French's house. A gentle tug, soothing words, promises of extra hot dogs, and Trixie follows him inside.

Archer French is a hoarder. The front part of the house is filled with stacked boxes like he recently moved in and hasn't had a chance to unpack yet. The air is stale with the smell of cigarette smoke. There are newspapers and magazines stacked in neat piles along the walls, and clothes, empty yogurt tubs, and canning jars tucked in between everything else. Hanging on one wall are collectible teaspoons. There's a lot of stuff in this house, but there are paths through the chaos and items grouped together by similarities. Purses with backpacks. Half-burned candles next to a bowl filled with matchboxes. The way Archer moves through the house, it's clear he knows where everything is. If Jimmy were to ask him for a specific item, he's sure Archer would be able to find it within seconds.

Jimmy stays in the living room while Archer disappears into the kitchen off to the left. A drawer opens. A loud thump as a heavy phone book drops onto a countertop.

"Have you been living in this neighborhood for a while?" Jimmy asks.

"A couple of years now."

"You like it out here?" He moves slowly through the living room, lifting trinkets, setting them down again. Trixie sticks close to his side. She sniffs the legs of chairs, noses a pile of magazines.

"It's quiet. And people mind their own business." There's tension in Archer's words, a warning.

Jimmy stops in front of a coat rack. A heavy wool coat hangs from one hook. There's mud on the sleeves, and one of the buttons is missing. Rausch asked him about a coat last year, had searched his closet looking for one similar to this, like something a Navy man might wear. Or someone who worked on a fishing boat. Jimmy runs his thumb over the torn threads where the button used to be, remembering how Rausch told him Cherish's killer wasn't as smart as Ted Bundy because he'd left something behind. In the last seconds of her death, she must have grabbed on to his coat and torn off the button. To the very end, she fought.

"Please don't touch my things."

Jimmy is so engrossed in his own thoughts, he doesn't hear Archer approach until he's standing right behind him. Trixie doesn't warn him either. She's found something interesting to sniff and paw at under the coat rack. She turns her head, trying to jam her whole face into the small gap between the feet of the coat rack and the floor.

"Sorry." Jimmy drops the coat. "I've never seen a jacket like this before. Where did you get it?"

Archer doesn't answer. He nudges Jimmy aside and tugs on the jacket sleeves, arranging the coat to whatever mysterious specifications he has. He brushes his hands over the lapels. After a few seconds, he turns to Jimmy and juts his sharp chin toward the kitchen. "Phone's in there."

Jimmy tugs on Trixie. Trixie tugs on a bit of fabric she found under the coat rack and out slips a pale yellow T-shirt. Jimmy reaches down to take it from Trixie's mouth. She lets go without a fight. Jimmy has only a few seconds to examine it before Archer French grabs it. Their hands brush momentarily. Archer's fingers are cold. Something predatory flashes in his eyes, a dark hunger that is quickly tamped down. Archer wads up the shirt in his hands, smiles, and in a sickly-sweet voice asks, "Do you want to call animal control, or should I?"

Jimmy says nothing about the brown stain he saw on the shirt right before Archer snatched it away, the splatter of dried blood ringing the torn collar.

He follows Archer into the kitchen, where the other man pulls open a slatted door beside the fridge and tosses the T-shirt into a laundry basket sitting on top of a washing machine. Archer closes the door again and gestures to a black phone sitting on a nearby counter. A phone book lies beside it, open to the phone number for animal control.

"They'll probably put her down," Archer says. "That's what they do to strays, you know. You'd probably save yourself a whole heap of trouble if you took her out to some field in the middle of the night and shot her yourself."

Archer holds Jimmy's gaze when he says it, as if he knows Jimmy's full of bullshit, or at least strongly suspects he's up to no good.

Jimmy glances down at Trixie, who's sitting on his foot now, panting. She looks up at him, and in her muddy brown eyes, he sees all the ways this could go wrong. But he's not ready to leave, not when he's so close to snagging the biggest story of his life. Face-to-face with a serial murderer, this is his chance to learn what turns a man into a monster.

Jimmy flashes a smile at Archer and gives an embarrassed shrug. "Any chance I could use your restroom? I think I drank too much coffee this morning."

Archer takes a second to answer, and in that space of time, Jimmy almost changes his mind. He's being given a chance to walk out of here alive, and he's not sure he'll get another one after this.

Archer points his finger down a darkened hallway off the kitchen that seems to extend forever. There is no end that Jimmy can see. It's a yawning black hole, alive with shadows.

"Second door on the right," Archer says.

Once Jimmy's eyes adjust to the dimness, he can see four doors, two on either side of the hallway, and all four are closed. Slivers of light scratch the floor, daylight slipping through the windows and creeping across the carpet. He moves toward the second door on the right. Trixie trails after him with her nose pressed to the floor, snuffling and sniffing. Jimmy ducks into the bathroom, which is crammed with buckets, toilet paper, and bottles of bleach lined up against the wall.

He searches through the medicine cabinet and under the sink but finds nothing interesting. He sticks his head out the door, listening to the sounds from the kitchen, clinking porcelain and water running, like Archer's washing dishes, then darts across the hallway to the room on the opposite side.

The room across from the bathroom appears to be Archer's bedroom. It's the least cluttered part of the house that Jimmy has seen so far, almost monk-like compared to the rest. A single bed has been pushed under the bare window. On a small nightstand beside it rests a lamp, an ashtray, and a cigarette pack. A braided rug covers a large section of the floor. There's a dresser on one wall, the top covered by an extensive collection of music boxes. On the other wall, paperback novels cram a tall bookshelf.

Jimmy hovers his hand over a bouquet of dried flowers lying on the top shelf in front of the books. The faded whites and purples of the petals are identical to the flowers found near Cherish Spalding's body. A flush of adrenaline runs through him. He's getting close. But a quick sweep through the rest of the room turns up nothing else but clothes and shoes in the closet and dust bunnies under the bed.

The next room Jimmy enters might have been considered a second bedroom if someone other than Archer French was living here. Instead, Archer seems to be using it for storage.

Several bookshelves are lined up the way they would be in a bookstore, sticking out from the walls rather than flush against them, creating a labyrinth-effect in the small room. Jimmy steps inside and pushes the door closed as soon as Trixie's through. He knows he's been gone too long and should get back to the kitchen before Archer comes looking for him, but the room seems to draw him in deeper.

He gets lost in it. Walking between the shelves, examining the trinkets on display. It's like a museum. There are old coins, arrowheads, shards of pottery, small animal bones bleached white and arranged with tender care. There are framed photographs of happy families. In one of the pictures, a young Archer French stands in front of a carousel next to a woman with features similar to Mary Andress. The woman has her arm around the boy. The boy's holding an ice cream cone, and it's melting. Vanilla cream drips onto the hot asphalt at his feet.

Farther back in the room, things become more cluttered and more strange. Clumps of hair, torn bits of clothes, a pile of fingernail clippings. There are metal filing cabinets tucked in one corner, but when Jimmy opens them, he finds they are empty, hollow shells storing nothing but air.

It's on the last shelf, the one closest to the window, that he finds what he came here for, what part of him was hoping not to find even as he knew it was inevitable. The mason jars are arranged to catch the sunlight filtering in through the window. A plush armchair faces the shelves. The clear fluid inside each jar glints and sparkles.

Trixie lets out a low whine and pulls sharply against the rope around her neck, refusing to go any closer to the chair and the shelf filled with jars. Jimmy drops the rope and steps toward the shelves, the hairs on the back of his neck lifting. He picks up one of the jars and turns it to get a better look at what's inside. The shape is unmistakable.

Cut from the mouth, the tongue is longer than he's ever seen it, stretched out in a disturbing manner, bobbing in the fluid, shifting as if it were still attached, moving around silent secrets and the many horror stories it could tell if given a chance.

He counts the jars. Eleven jars, eleven tongues. Each lid is labeled with two letters. Initials, he realizes as he finds jars labeled LR and CS and NT.

He checks each one but finds none with the letters M and B.

A floorboard creaks. When Jimmy turns around, it's Archer French's shadow he sees first—a slim blade cutting across the floor.

"Find what you're looking for?" Archer steps into the room.

"I guess I got a little turned around." Jimmy lets out an uncomfortable laugh.

Archer doesn't buy it. He takes a step closer. "Why are you here?" Another step. The floor groans under his weight. "And don't give me any more bullshit about a lost dog. Why are you snooping through my things?"

"Margot Buchanan." The name slips from Jimmy's mouth before he can stop it. "You have all the others here." He flicks his eyes to the jars and then back to Archer. "Where is Margot?"

Archer tilts his head, and a furrow forms on his brow. He seems to be thinking over the name, tracing it back along some long-forgotten thread of memory. A look of recognition flickers over his face, a whisper of a smile that quickly disappears.

"Does anyone know you're here?" Archer asks, and the tone of his voice has changed, switched to something low and menacing.

Jimmy glances at the window that's right next to him. It's painted shut. Cobwebs stretch across the glass. Desiccated bodies of flies litter the window sill. He could break the glass with his elbow, try and shimmy his way out, but he knows Archer will move faster and drag him back inside. Plus, there's no way in hell Jimmy's going to leave Trixie alone with this monster. She wandered off when Jimmy's attention was focused on the jars. He scans the room but doesn't see her.

A smile splits Archer's face. "Wow. You really didn't think this through, did you? What were you hoping to accomplish by barging into my house like this? What did you think was going to happen?"

Archer takes another step closer. He's blocking the door and Jimmy's exit, but his hands are empty. Archer isn't that much bigger than Jimmy. If this comes down to a physical fight, it's not entirely clear who would win. Jimmy wants better odds than fifty-fifty. He grabs a jar off the shelf at random and lifts it high in the air.

"Put that back." Archer lurches toward Jimmy, his teeth bared in a grimace.

Jimmy hurls the jar at Archer. The jar deflects off the other man's chest, drops to the floor, and shatters. The liquid sprays in an arc. The tongue slides a few feet and disappears under one of the shelves.

A groan creaks from Archer's lips. He seems torn about whether to grab Jimmy or rescue the tongue. Taking advantage of his hesitation, Jimmy grabs another jar and throws this one on the floor, too. The glass shatters. Archer cries out again, a strangled sound like an animal cornered. He drops to his hands and knees, scrambling to grab the tongue within reach before crawling toward the bookshelf to try and rescue the other one. In doing so, he leaves space for Jimmy to escape.

Jimmy darts toward the door and the hallway beyond. He calls for Trixie, who appears from behind one of the shelves. She moves faster than Jimmy and gets under his feet. He stumbles and steps on her paw. She yelps and feints away from him. Even though she's almost a year old now, she's still all bumbling puppy, and sometimes her feet get ahead of her, and she didn't mean to, she didn't, but it happens anyway. She trips him, and in those few, clumsy seconds, Archer French catches up to them.

A hand bloodied from broken glass slams down onto Jimmy's shoulders and spins him around. He swings his arms up to protect his face, but he's too slow. Archer's fist connects to his cheek and knocks him backward. His head slams onto the floor. For an instant, the world goes black and numb, then he blinks himself awake again. Something hard jabs into the small of his back.

Trixie is nearby barking, barking, then her barks turn to howls. Then there's a sharp yelp, and Trixie falls silent. This gets Jimmy off the floor. He pushes up to a sitting position, head spinning. He might vomit, but he's not going to let this bastard hurt his dog.

He looks around and sees he's about ten feet from the front door. Archer's standing a few feet from him, distracted with something under the couch. Trixie, Jimmy realizes as he hears her now, growling and snapping her teeth. She's wedged herself into the small space beneath the couch somehow. Archer has one arm shoved under as he tries to pull her out.

Jimmy rises to his feet, swaying from the blow he took to the head. He reaches out for something to hold on to, afraid he's going to fall again, and grabs on to a department store mannequin. She rocks on her pedestal, unsteady.

Archer turns to look at the noise and, forgetting Trixie, leaps to his feet to come after Jimmy. Jimmy shoves the mannequin at Archer and lunges toward the door. All he has to do is get outside, get out of this nightmare carnival of a house thick with dust that shimmers gold in the air, thick with the ghosts of dead girls. Get outside, get in his car, drive until he finds a payphone, call the police.

He shouts for Trixie. The beagle scrambles out from under the couch and charges toward Jimmy.

He flings open the door, and she's through it before he even has time to blink. A streak of brown and white fur, she's halfway down the driveway while Jimmy's still on the front porch, feeling like he's moving in slow-motion. The blow to the head may have done more damage than he thought. He doesn't move automatically. He has to think, *lift your right foot, now your left,* and even then, the muscles are slow to react. Static crackles at the edge of his vision.

A woman comes out of the house across the street and starts to walk down her driveway toward the mailbox. Trixie runs toward her, barking. Jimmy shouts for help, but his words are cut short as a hand grabs him and yanks him back inside the house. The door slams shut. Archer shoves his full weight into Jimmy's back, pressing him up against the wood, laying his arm across his neck, the heaviness of it like a thousand-pound boa constrictor. Jimmy struggles to push back and break free, but Archer keeps him there against the door.

"You son of a bitch." Archer's voice is a rasping whisper in his ear. His smoky breath flames hot against Jimmy's cheek. "Did you really think you could come into my house, wreck my things, and get away with it? You think I don't know who you are? I know you,

Jimmy Eagan. I know what you call me. I know who you think I am."

Through the other side of the door, Jimmy can hear Trixie barking and howling, scratching at the wood, and this gives him a second burst of energy. He throws his elbow back and connects with Archer's ribs. The other man sucks in a sharp breath but doesn't ease up. The blow just makes him angrier. He leans more weight against Jimmy's shoulders. Something in Jimmy's back pops.

Archer is stronger than he looks. Rage and desperation twist into steel fists. He spins Jimmy, so they're face-to-face, then jerks him away from the door and heaves him to the floor in the center of the living room like he weighs nothing. Jimmy tries to crawl in the opposite direction toward the kitchen, remembering another door there, hoping it leads to the garage. But Archer is on top of him in seconds.

He pins Jimmy down, keeping him trapped, even as Jimmy thrashes and fights and tries to break free. Archer encircles both hands around Jimmy's neck. His fingers become steel bands pressing hard against his throat, cutting off all air. He takes his time, loosening his hold enough for Jimmy to suck in a little bit of air before clamping tight again, giving Jimmy a flicker of hope before snatching it away. Sparks flash in his vision.

This is how it was for the August girls, Jimmy thinks, as he feels himself slipping into darkness.

It's awful, dying this way, slow and unrelenting, the face of his killer pressed so close they are breathing the same air. He can see the hate in Archer French's ice-blue eyes and a glimmer, a glint, the slightest reflection of another man.

Jimmy can see himself in Archer's eyes.

He can see all his regrets, the pride and ego that brought him here, the future he will never have, all the stories he'll never tell, the promises he made, broken now. He thinks of Brett, of how he might be falling in love with her, he's pretty sure he is, but it's too late to tell her now. He should have called her, he realizes. Before he came here, he should have called her and told her exactly what he was planning. She would have talked him out of this idiotic decision to face the Ophelia Killer alone. She would have come with him if she knew where he was going, and with his final conscious thought, Jimmy can't decide if that would have made things better or worse.

CHAPTER 19

From somewhere far off, Jimmy Eagan hears someone calling his name.

A woman.

He turns his head toward the voice but sees only a long, dark tunnel with no end. He blinks, and a fleck of gold light appears. The tiniest of dots. A dust mote, a firefly. It will take him forever to reach it.

The woman continues to call for him. The speck of light grows larger until it swallows him. He shrinks from it, groaning. He blinks, and shapes begin to materialize around him. The edges of a window frame. The sharp line where the wall meets the ceiling. The gauzy soft flutter of a curtain. A metal pole stands next to him, a plastic tube feeding into his arm. And sitting in a chair next to the bed is Brett.

She smiles at him.

"Welcome back." Her voice is soft and low.

"What happened?" It hurts to talk. Now that he's noticing, a lot of him hurts. The last thing he remembers is being in Archer French's house, running toward the door, tripping over Trixie. He blinks, and the images change. No. The last thing he remembers is Archer French's hands wrapped around his throat. His own hand lifts, touching the rough patch of skin where a beard is beginning to grow. He wonders how long he's been lying in this hospital bed, but he doesn't have the energy to say the words out loud.

All he can manage is a single, rasping sound. "Trixie?"

"She's okay. She's fine. Better than you." Brett's smile is tense, and her voice splinters when she says, "What the hell were you thinking, Jimmy? Going into that madman's house alone?"

She exhales and drops her head into her hands. Her brown hair falls in front of her face, and Jimmy realizes this is the first time he's seen her wear it loose. She always keeps it in a ponytail or a low bun against the back of her neck. He wants to reach out and touch it, tuck it behind her ear, comfort her, but when he tries to move, pain burns through his entire body.

He hisses through clenched teeth. Brett snaps her head up. "What is it? Do you need me to call the doctor?"

"No," he says. "No, I'm fine."

"You're not fine." She rises from the chair and moves around his bed, fussing over him, tucking the sheets tighter around his legs as she talks. "You were technically dead for ten minutes. If Trixie hadn't kept barking her damn head off, if that neighbor across the street hadn't seen you and called the police right away—for fuck's sake, Jimmy."

She straightens, settles her hands on her hips, and cocks her head to look at him. A frown teases the corners of her mouth. "I thought we'd lost you. You weren't breathing when the paramedics got to you. By some miracle, though, they brought you back. You're damn lucky, you know that?"

"Damn stupid, is what you're really thinking." He coughs on the words.

Brett shakes her head and lifts a plastic pitcher from the tray beside the bed. She fills a small plastic cup, sticks a straw in it, and holds it near Jimmy's mouth. "Drink."

He sips the tepid water. It hurts to swallow, but he takes another sip because the water soothes his parched throat enough for him to say, "I'm sorry. I wanted to be sure."

"You wanted your goddamn story."

He doesn't deny it.

Brett sets the cup back down on the tray and returns to the chair beside his bed, flopping into it with a heavy sigh. "Well?"

"Well, what?"

"Are you going to tell me what the hell happened? The last time I talked to you, you were still in Crestwood trying to come up with a name. Next thing I know, there's a call coming over the radio saying some dumb ass reporter's got himself in a heap of shit." She leans forward and rests her hands on the edge of the hospital bed. "Is it him, Jimmy? Archer French? Is he the Ophelia Killer?"

He closes his eyes, remembering the collection of jars glinting in the sunlight streaming through the window, how all of the August girls were accounted for except one.

"She wasn't there," he says.

Brett's eyebrows pinch in confusion. "What are you talking about?"

He explains about the jars, the tongues, the initials. "There were no jars labeled MB. At least, none that I found."

Her shoulders hunch higher as she folds slightly into herself.

"It doesn't mean anything," Jimmy rushes on, trying to sit up, but a bolt of pain pushes him back against the pillows.

Brett's frown deepens. "Take it easy. You just went through hell."

"He was in Crestwood that summer, though," Jimmy says. "And the way she was found, it seems pretty clear to me. Even if he didn't keep—" He stops himself from saying it but quickly adds, "He killed her, Brett. I'm sure of it. We got our man."

Brett checks her watch in a way that makes Jimmy think she's avoiding looking at him. "He's being interrogated as we speak. So hopefully, they'll pull some answers from him soon."

"You should be there," he says.

She laughs, a bitter sound. "And miss out on lecturing you about your life choices?"

"Let me guess," Jimmy says. "Rausch wouldn't let you anywhere near the interview room?"

Brett's expression is all the answer he needs.

"Anyway," she says with a shrug. "The investigation is over now. Like you said, we got our man. The special unit is being disbanded. They're trimming the fat. I'm back with the sheriff's department tomorrow. Back out on patrol."

Before Jimmy can ask how she feels about that, there's a sharp knock on the door, and a nurse enters to check Jimmy's vitals. She tells him that he'll be sore for a while. His throat is swollen, so it will hurt to eat and swallow, but he should make a full recovery. She tells him they're keeping him overnight for monitoring, but once the doctor has a look at him and gives the okay, he should be able to head home as early as tomorrow morning.

After the nurse leaves, Brett scowls at Jimmy. "All that trouble and you only have to spend two nights in the hospital. Damn lucky," she repeats.

He starts to apologize again, but she takes his hand, squeezes it. "Next time you decide to play hero, at least call me first, okay?"

He nods, and his eyes flutter closed as exhaustion sweeps him into a heavy sleep.

When Jimmy wakes again, Brett is gone. In her chair sits Detective Michael Rausch. He's staring at the wall, a scowl etched into the stone of his face. Jimmy shifts in the bed, and Rausch's gaze swivels to him.

"You here to apologize?" Jimmy goads. "Tell me I was right."

Rausch tenses. His hands curl to fists on the armrests of the chair. "How did you find Archer French?"

"I looked for him. I asked the right questions."

He feels a little more rested, stronger now, too. But it still hurts to talk, and he wants Rausch to disappear. He longs for Brett to be sitting in that chair again, watching over him.

"Don't play games with me, Slim-Jim," Rausch says.

Jimmy leans his head back against the pillow and lifts his eyes toward the ceiling.

Rausch scoots the chair right up next to the hospital bed and bends close to Jimmy. "You might think you can hide from everyone else, but you can't hide from me. You worked with Archer, is that it? The two of you were in this together, but what happened? You got tired of sharing the glory? He threatened to turn you in? But how did you convince him to take the fall?"

"You're out of your mind, Rausch." It takes all of Jimmy's efforts to push himself up in bed, so he's sitting tall and facing the detective directly. "Just because I did something you weren't able or willing to do, doesn't make me a criminal. He would have gone on killing if I hadn't stopped him."

He falls back against the pillows again, panting, exhausted.

Rausch rises out of the chair, a smirk tugging on his mouth. He shakes his head, then takes a notepad from his jacket pocket along with a pen and sets both down on Jimmy's legs. "Archer French gave us a pretty thorough confession after we laid out all the evidence we had against him. Between him and your boss, we were able to piece together a pretty good timeline of events, but I'm still going to need your statement. When you're feeling up to it."

He taps his fingers twice on the notepad. He pauses in the doorway on the way out and casts a glance over his shoulder at Jimmy. "And remember, Slim-Jim, I'm watching you. I'll always be watching you."

The nightmares start two weeks after Jimmy gets out of the hospital. The details change from dream to dream, but the feeling is the same: terror. A hand coming out of the darkness, pulling Jimmy down. Jimmy is walking along a sidewalk, rain sputtering around him, when suddenly the ground gives way, and he's falling, falling. A girl screams in the distance, and Jimmy tries to run in her direction, tries to save her, but his legs get stuck in quicksand or break into a thousand pieces.

He wakes in a panic, sweating and unable to catch his breath. The sheets tangle around his body, choking him. But Trixie is always there to calm him down again. She nuzzles her head under his arm and presses the entire length of her body against his. Her warmth comforts him enough he's usually able to fall right back to sleep.

But sometimes he can't, and it's nights like these when he loads Trixie in the car and drives in circles through the countryside, watching the shadows for movement, for something amiss.

Archer French is being held in prison without bail until his next hearing. He's of no danger to anyone now. Still, Jimmy drives. He keeps his eyes open. He watches the shadows, knowing other monsters lurk in the dark, predators like Archer French, who are biding their time, waiting to kill.

Chapter 20

On a hot night in August, nearly three months after French's arrest, Jimmy wakes from another nightmare. He grabs Trixie's leash and heads out for a drive.

He's cruising down a two-lane highway near Valentine Creek, scanning the fields and gravel shoulders, when he sees flashing blue and red lights in his rearview mirror.

He isn't speeding. He's not drunk. He doesn't think he ran any stop signs. He pulls to the side of the road. The patrol car pulls up behind him, lights still swirling. The officer, a shadow in the headlights, walks slowly toward his vehicle.

Jimmy grips the wheel, thinking it's Rausch who pulled him over. Rausch with his wrong theories and personal vendetta. This dark highway with no one around for miles—the detective could do whatever he wants to Jimmy and get away with it.

But the silhouette standing at his driver's side door is slimmer and shorter than Rausch, and the voice is feminine and familiar. "I thought that was you."

Jimmy relaxes his grip on the steering wheel. He hasn't seen Brett since that first night in the hospital. He thought about calling her several times, but whenever it came down to actually picking up the phone, he always lost his nerve.

"What are you doing out here?" she asks, glancing around the empty farmland.

"I couldn't sleep."

"He can't hurt anyone anymore, you know." Her voice is quiet in the dark. "There won't be another August girl this year, Jimmy. There won't be one next year, either. You should go home and read a book. Or write one, for God's sake. Just stop wasting your time out here chasing shadows."

Jimmy stares through the windshield. A moth flutters in the glare of his headlights.

"So, listen." Brett's tone shifts to something more playful. "If I didn't know any better, I'd think you were avoiding me."

He turns to look at her. "What do you mean?"

She bends so her face is framed by the window, then she reaches her hand inside to scratch Trixie's head. "Hey, girl. How have you been?" She smiles at Jimmy. "I've been down at the bar every Thursday. Thought for sure I'd run into you there at some point."

He feels his cheeks grow hot and is grateful for the cover of darkness. "Oh, well, I thought since you weren't with the special unit anymore—"

"The special unit is over, Jimmy. But that doesn't mean our friendship has to be."

"Right."

She studies him a moment and says, "You at least owe me one more drink."

"Oh? How's that?"

"Without me, you would have never tracked down Archer French." She straightens and adjusts her utility belt. "So, I'll see you Thursday afternoon? My shift ends at four."

Jimmy nods.

Brett pats the roof of his car twice and walks away.

Jimmy shows up to the bar a little before four on Thursday, thinking he'll beat Brett. But she's already there, waiting for him in their usual booth, their favorite confessional near the jukebox. Two pints of beer and a plate of greasy fries sit on the table in front of her.

He starts to walk over, but the bartender intercepts him and insists on shaking his hand. He tells Jimmy to bring Trixie in with him anytime he wants. She's a hero as much as he is. Everyone's heard about Jimmy's confrontation with the Ophelia Killer by now. The story's been plastered on the front-page of the *Statesman Journal* for weeks, thanks to Tadd. Other papers picked it up, too, but Jimmy's first-hand account is exclusive to the one he writes for. Jimmy's never seen his editor as happy as he's been for the past three months.

Jimmy frees himself from the bartender's grip and drops down onto the vinyl bench across from Brett. He sneaks a fry into his mouth.

"So. You're a big shot celebrity now," she says.

"Hardly."

"Too good for the likes of us ordinary people."

"I'm here, aren't I?" He keeps his voice light, teasing her, as he grabs another fry.

"Yeah, well, I was starting to think you weren't coming," she says, but there's no anger in her voice either. She relaxes against the bench, studying his face.

"You look good," she says. "Better than when I saw you three months ago."

"Has it really been that long?"

She shrugs.

"Well, I don't have any permanent damage," Jimmy says, reaching for his beer. He doesn't mention the nightmares or the way his throat sometimes hurts for no reason. "How is it back at the sheriff's department?"

The offices the Salem Police were using for their special investigations unit are empty now. There's a For Lease sign in the front window.

"Boring." Brett shrugs. "I thought maybe I could talk the sheriff into giving me a promotion, but so far, there haven't been any openings."

"You could always apply to a different department? Portland is always looking for good police."

She laughs. "Portland? Why the hell would I go to Portland?"

"I'm moving there next month."

She looks surprised, then angry. "Why?"

"Got a job offer from the *Oregonian*. It's more money, bigger stories. Hard to turn that down." Plus, he needs a change in scenery. New roads that don't lead him to the dumping grounds of dead girls. Shadows that aren't so twisted. Sleep that doesn't give him nightmares. He doesn't know if he can really leave the August girls behind, but he wants to try.

"Good for you. Congratulations." Brett's smile doesn't reach her eyes. She seems sad about his news, maybe just disappointed.

"I've had some publishers contact me, too," he says. "They're interested in my story, of how I tracked down Archer, the whole ordeal, how I survived"

"That's great, Jimmy."

"Is it?"

"You don't want to do it?"

"I do, I think I do. I just wonder if maybe it would be better to put the whole thing behind me, forget it ever happened."

"But it did happen. Maybe instead of forgetting, you need to face it head-on. Tell the whole story, and it will stop haunting you."

"Where'd you hear that from?"

"It's something my grandpa used to say to me. After my sister died. Whenever I was having a hard time with school or my parents or whatever. I was always pushing my feelings down, pushing it all away, and he sat me down one day and said that was the worst thing I could do. He told me that yes, this world is cruel, that it will do its damnedest to try and break me. He said the things that happened to me could either turn me calloused, hard, and mean, or I could open up, let the hurts in, and then turn them into something useful, something that made me kind and compassionate. I don't know." She laughs softly and shakes her head. "I never completely understood what he was trying to say or how to do that. You know? How to stay tough here..." She taps her finger against her temple. "While also staying soft here." Her finger moves to her chest, touching above her heart. "But he said that's how you survive the things life throws at you, that's how you stay sane. By remembering your humanity. It's the only way to make anything meaningful from this tragic mess of a world."

Brett smiles across the table at Jimmy. He smiles back at her and starts to lean closer, the words forming in his mouth. He's going to ask her to come with him to Portland. He's going to tell her how he feels. But as his courage is building, she reaches for a french fry and changes the subject.

"I didn't want to ask you while you were in the hospital, it didn't seem right. But I've been wondering, I can't stop thinking about it. When you were with French? When you were at his house? Did he tell you about Margot? Did he say anything to you about killing her?"

Jimmy shakes his head. "I'm sorry, Brett. He admitted to being in Crestwood, but that was the closest I got."

She slumps back in the booth, disappointed. "I should have known it wouldn't be that easy."

Their eyes meet, and he sees his own doubts reflected back to him. She knows something he doesn't. He stays silent, waiting her out.

Finally, she says, "I could get in deep shit telling you this. Rausch isn't making this public yet, so maybe don't make an article out of it just yet, but Archer is swearing up and down and sideways that he didn't kill Margot. He confessed to the other eleven women during the interrogation. All the ones we knew about. Lydia and Cherish and Natalie, the others. The ones whose tongues were…" She shakes the image from her head. "He admits to killing all eleven of those women, but every time they ask him about Margot, he says he didn't do it. He says it wasn't him."

"He's a liar, Brett. A psychopath."

"Yes, but I keep thinking, what if he's telling the truth? What if he didn't kill Margot? What if someone else did?" She looks sickened at the thought of it. A shudder rolls through her, and she says, "Never mind, it's stupid. Of course, it was him. He's just playing games with us, trying to keep some leverage or something for the trial."

"Will there even be a trial? If he's confessed to everything?"

"There will be a sentencing hearing, at least. But I don't know, I think I need to try and move on. Accept that he's the one who killed Margot. I need to try and find some closure here." She runs her hand over her face. "Is that even possible? She was my big sister, my best friend. Every time I think about what happened to her, what he did—" She swallows the rest.

"It'll get easier," he says and instantly wishes he could take it back. "Sorry, that was a stupid thing to say."

She shakes her empty pint glass at him. "Buy me another, and I'll find it in my heart to forgive you."

Two hours later, they walk out to the parking lot together. Jimmy lets Trixie out of the car, and Brett crouches to say hi to the beagle, who can't stop moving. She wiggles and wags and bumps her nose against Brett's arms and legs and elbows and anything else she can find.

Brett gives the dog a good, long scratch, then stands up and dusts her hands off on her pants. "Well, Jimmy, I guess this is goodbye."

"What do you mean? Like goodbye goodbye?"

"Well, you're moving to Portland, right? Out with the old, in with the new. A fresh start and all of that."

"I'm taking a new job, Bretty, moving to a new apartment, not abandoning my entire life. It's less than an hour's drive from Portland to Salem. My mom's still here. You're still here. I'll probably be back here visiting so often, you'll get sick of me."

She studies him a moment, then nods like she's made up her mind.

"See you next Thursday, then?" She sticks her hand out like they're negotiating a business deal.

To do the kind of work Jimmy wants to do, to chase monsters, to write the violent truth, he has to hold on to the parts of this life that are good, and Brett is good, perhaps the best thing that's happened to him in a long time.

He grabs her hand and pulls her forward into an embrace. She stiffens a second, then relaxes against him and speaks softly into his ear. "I'm going to miss you, Jimmy."

"I'm just a phone call away, Bretty," he says, holding her a little tighter.

Brett ends the hug first. Before she leaves, she bends to give Trixie one more scratch on the head and says, "Be a good girl and keep an eye on him for me, okay?"

Trixie's tongue flops from her mouth in a wide, conspiratorial grin.

Brett shoves her hands in her pockets and starts to walk away. Over her shoulder, she says, "Stay out of trouble."

"All the best stories come from trouble," Jimmy calls after her. She shakes her head and lifts her hand in a wave.

Twenty minutes later, Jimmy turns onto the road leading to Crocker Creek. Though it's after six now, it's still summer; the sun won't set for another two hours. He parks near the spot where Cherish Spalding's body was found and lets Trixie out of the car. The dog takes off ahead of him, parting the tall grass, sniffing in a sporadic zig-zag, nose snuffling the soft earth. Jimmy takes his time crossing the field. He stops when he gets to the trees, his toes on the edge where the long shadows and copper sunlight meet.

Birds whistle and chirp in the canopy. The creek where she laid for hours burbles and mutters to itself. Jimmy waits for something to happen. The air is still. The sun tilts low to the horizon, but still warms the skin on the back of his neck and arms. He waits, but nothing happens, and after a while, he's not sure why he came. To say goodbye, to apologize, to try and reckon with the happiness he feels alongside his grief. If not for the August girls, he would not have found Trixie. He would not have found Brett, either. There is infinite pain in this world, loss so deep a person could drown in it. But there is beauty, too, and hope if you know where to look.

As Jimmy turns to go back to the car, he whistles for Trixie. There's a rustle in the dry grass, and then she is at his side, bounding through a sea of white, purple, and yellow wildflowers blooming all around them.

Acknowledgements

A quick but heartfelt thanks to Alisa Callos for being my second pair of eyes, Ken Brayton for suggesting Trixie make her entrance a few scenes earlier, Caroline Starr Rose for cheering the loudest while reminding me to take breaks, and Ryan Geary for his steadfast belief in my wildest daydreams.

And extra thanks to you, Dear Reader. For always being excited to hear from me. I hope you have as much fun reading this one as I had writing it!

About the Author

Valerie Geary is the author of several books, including the Brett Buchanan Mystery Series and *Crooked River*, her debut and a finalist for the Oregon Book Award. She lives in the Pacific Northwest with her husband and a rescue dog named Charlie Waffles. Connect with her on Facebook, Instagram, or YouTube to find out what she's reading. Or sign up for her monthly newsletter to receive discounts, free books, and a behind-the-scenes look at her writing and hiking life: www.valeriegeary.com

Someone in this town is keeping a deadly secret.

The man who claims to know the truth about a
decades-old murder is dead.

For Detective Brett Buchanan, the hunt for her sister's
killer is just beginning…

PLEASE ENJOY AN EXCERPT FROM

ON A DARK TIDE
BRETT BUCHANAN MYSTERY SERIES
BOOK 1

Chapter 1

Brett hadn't seen any signs of rats in the four months she'd been living with her grandmother in the big house overlooking Sculpin Bay, but Amma insisted she heard them. They were keeping her awake at night, she said. Furry little bastards would chew apart the attic if someone didn't stop them. And by someone, she meant Brett.

Amma was afraid of the ladder that unfolded from the ceiling, worried that if she tried to climb the narrow rungs, she would fall, break her hip, and lie for days in agony until someone found her. If someone found her. A woman who lives alone dies alone, Amma liked to say with a bitter twist of her coral-tinted lips. But she wasn't alone anymore, Brett reminded her nearly every day.

In June, Brett had uprooted her entire life to come and live with Amma in Crestwood, a salt-encrusted fleck of nowhere town in Washington, less than an hour's drive from the Canadian border. Part of their arrangement was that Brett could stay on rent-free indefinitely as long as she helped out with the things Pop used to do. Like raking leaves, and cleaning gutters, and climbing into the attic on her day off to set traps for imaginary rats.

As far as Brett could tell, no one had been in the attic since Pop died of a heart attack five years ago. A thick layer of dust covered the beams and eaves and boxes stacked underneath. She wiggled a trap into the narrow space between an old wardrobe and the wall. Once all the traps were in place, she worked her way back toward the open hatch, weaving through the cluttered odds-and-ends her grandparents had accumulated during their sixty years together. At some point, she and Amma would have to go through it all and decide what was worth saving.

Downstairs, a door slammed. Brett startled at the sound and bumped into a stack of boxes. The top one fell, and the lid opened. Cameras, film canisters, and stacks of curled, faded photographs spilled across the attic floor.

Brett sat a minute listening, in case Amma needed help. She'd been losing her balance recently, tripping over uneven thresholds and her own feet. *It's nothing*, she'd say, waving away Brett's concern. *I'm getting clumsy in my old age, that's all.*

When no other sounds came from downstairs, Brett assumed everything was fine.

During the summer months, Amma took her breakfast of black coffee and toast onto the back patio, where she would watch cormorants glide across the glinting surface of Sculpin Bay and scan the horizon for whales. Though it was mid-October now, and most mornings were too cold to sit out on the porch for long, Amma would sometimes wrap herself in a sweater and do it anyway. According to her, the murmur of water against the pebbled beach calmed her nerves.

Brett returned her focus to cleaning up the mess she'd made. She put the cameras and lenses back into the box without much thought but took her time with the photographs.

Many were black-and-white, abstract glimpses of light and shapes, her grandfather dabbling with his artistic side. She took a minute flipping through a small stack of pictures where the subjects were people rather than buildings and landscapes. Pictures of Amma and Pop together and impossibly young. A baby in Amma's lap grinning toothless, followed by more photos of the same baby in a frilly, white dress. Then in a diaper, crawling across the dock. Then in a sailboat with Pop. Then sitting in the grass outside this very house that hadn't changed much over the years with its wrap-around porch, Victorian turret, and wind vane shaped like a whale. The baby in these pictures was Brett's mother. The cowlick curl over her forehead was the same cowlick Brett had been trying to tame her whole life. In a later picture, her mother's cowlick had disappeared, her hair turned honey-blond and soft, her eyes mischievous. The resemblance to Brett's older sister was startling enough, she did a double-take. She had never realized how much Margot looked like their mother.

As girls, Brett and Margot spent every summer from the Fourth of July to Labor Day in Crestwood with their grandparents. Wild days, golden days, she remembered them as glinting and saturated bright, until the summer of 1964 when their lives shattered. Brett hadn't thought she would ever return to Crestwood after what happened that summer. Yet here she was twenty years later, and though her heart was no less broken than the day they found Margot's body, she had at least gotten better at pretending.

The smell of burning toast wafted into the attic.

"Amma?" Brett called down. "Is everything okay?"

When she received no response, Brett abandoned the rest of the mess to pick up later. She climbed down the ladder and went into the kitchen, where gray smoke billowed from the toaster. Brett fumbled with the handle until the damn thing finally popped. She pinched a corner of the charred toast and tossed it into the sink. A flush of water and the smoke dissipated, though the stench of it hung thick in the air.

"Amma?" Brett called out again.

From the small radio on the counter, two pundits discussed tomorrow's second presidential debate between Reagan and Mondale. A mug beside it had been filled to the brim with coffee and left to go cold. Brett flicked off the radio.

The double french doors leading out to the back porch hung wide open. A cool breeze blew through. Brett slipped on a pair of rain boots, grabbed Amma's favorite sky-blue cardigan from its hook beside the door, and went outside. She stepped off the porch and walked across the backyard that sloped to a pebbled beach.

Amma, a petite silhouette against a damp gray October sky, stood on the beach a few steps from the dock and a small boathouse, painted the same cheerful yellow as the main house. A fourteen-foot sailboat bobbed in the water, tugging against the ropes that kept it lashed to the dock. Amma's back was to Brett, but she wasn't looking out over the bay. Her head was tilted, and she was staring at her feet. Not at her feet, Brett realized as she walked closer, but at a pile of wet clothes. She quickened her pace. Even this far away, she could tell that what had washed up this morning was more than rags.

She stepped off the lawn. Pebbles crunched underfoot.

Without looking up, Amma flapped her hand and said, "Don't come any closer, Brett, dear. This isn't something you need to see."

Brett grabbed Amma and pulled her away from the body.

Small waves rocked the man gently. He was on his stomach, face pressed into the rocks, his arms trapped beneath him. The skin of his neck, visible above his shirt collar, was bloated and splotched purple. Working as a sheriff's deputy for the past ten years, and now as a detective, Brett had seen enough bodies to know without needing to bend close or check his pulse that this man was unmistakably dead.

She swung her gaze along the beach and out across the water, looking for a wrecked boat or something else to explain how he'd come to wash up on this particular shore. There was nothing out of the ordinary. An empty stretch of sand and stone, the soft pull of the tide, a seagull eyeing them from the roof of the boathouse.

Brett turned her attention back to Amma, who was shivering so hard her teeth chattered. She had been out here only a few minutes, but the thin linen pants and short-sleeved blouse she was wearing did little to protect her from the mist and light breeze coming off the water. They were close enough to the shoreline that waves rolled over her bare feet. The cuffs of her pants were soaked past the ankle.

Brett spread the cardigan over Amma's shoulders. "What are you even doing out here?"

"I was going to take the boat out for a jaunt." Amma wrapped the cardigan tight around herself.

"You don't have any shoes on."

Amma looked at her feet, confusion rippling across her face, then she blinked and straightened her shoulders. A frown tugged at the corners of her mouth. "A man is dead, Brett. I hardly think now is the time to hassle me about my choice of attire."

"I wasn't trying to hassle you. I just—"

"I'm going to call the police." Amma spun away from her and marched up the hill toward the house. The long hem of her cardigan a fluttering scrap of sky against the gray mist and steel-colored clouds.

ON A DARK TIDE is available to purchase through all major retailers or you can buy the book directly from my online store.

To receive new release information, discounts, and more, sign up to be a VIP Reader today!

valeriegeary.com